EARTHLY REWARDS

*An anthology of fiction,
poetry & experimental writing*

Previous anthologies from thi wurd

Tales From a Cancelled Country (2015)
Work in Progress (2016)
Alternating Current (2022)

EARTHLY REWARDS

www.thi-wurd.com

First published in Glasgow, Scotland in 2024 by thi wurd

This edition first published in this format 2024 by thi wurd

Copyright ©

The moral right of the contributors to be identified
as the authors of their work has been asserted by
them in accordance with the Copyright, Designs
and Patents Act 1988

All rights reserved. No part of this publication may be reproduced, stored or
transmitted in any form without the express written permission of the publisher

ISBN 978-1-8381030-6-4

British Library Cataloguing-in-Publication Data
A catalogue record for this book is available from the British Library

Cover Image by Lorna Robertson
Copyright © Lorna Robertson

Illustrations by Andrew Cranston
Copyright © Andrew Cranston

Cover design by Maeve Redmond
Cover photography by Fabio Rebelo Paiva

Designed and typeset by
Palimpsest Book Production Limited, Falkirk, Stirlingshire

Printed and bound by CPI Group (UK) Ltd, Croydon, CR0 4YY

Massive thanks to Lorna Robertson and Andrew Cranston. Their art lifts this anthology to another level. We've been extremely lucky to collaborate with these artists, and everyone at thi wurd appreciates their kindness and generosity.

We assembled a truly gifted team to research, edit and proofread. Thanks to Rachel Carmichael, Rowan Groat, Barbara McLean, Katie Paterson and Jess Smith. Collectively they brought so much artistry, intelligence and knowledge to this edition.

Thanks to Maeve Redmond for designing the cover and for giving such a wonderful look to this book.

Our thanks also go to Justine Fourny, Kate McAllan and Bethany Spain for their invaluable assistance on several stories.

Andrew Cattanach was on hand to help: as always, his wisdom and insight were vital.

Thanks to Marie McQuade for her support of thi wurd and for setting up the visual art collaborations that have been game-changers for us.

Finally, a special thanks to Pamela McLean for taking on such a large editing, proofreading and administrative role, for charting the journey this project took, and for the part she played in bringing *Earthly Rewards* into being.

This book is dedicated to our friend,
Ralph Mackenzie (1986–2023).

Ralph did so much to support and elevate our work, building our website and designing the look of thi wurd online. We are thankful for his creativity and selflessness, and he will always be a part of what we do.

Introduction

Alan McMunnigall

It's a January night and rain is drumming on the windows. I'm listening to a Bob Dylan concert from 1963, thinking about how magical it is that a recording from over 60 years ago is making me feel such strong emotions. And then I'm thinking about art that endures. I wonder if this new anthology could endure and connect with people 60 years from now? Because the hope is always to create enduring art. Of course, we have no real say in what lasts and what falls away through the years. But today, when I reread this work from start to finish, I knew we had put together something special.

The idea is always for each wurd publication to be distinct: for each magazine, book or anthology to be an artistic evolution, holding its own ground. It wasn't until after we'd sequenced all the work that I fully understood the shape and power of this collection. Thematically and artistically it goes places we haven't gone before – it has its own style and identity. Yes, *Earthly Rewards* has its heart in Glasgow, but it branches out to include contributions from writers and artists in many different places, countries and continents.

While distinct and individual, this book builds upon the work in our previous anthology *Alternating Current*, which was launched in November 2022 to a sold-out crowd at Civic House in Glasgow. At that event we had 200 people in attendance to hear readings and live music. The audience had travelled from across the UK, Ireland, mainland Europe and even the USA. The evening concluded with guest reader Bernard MacLaverty giving a typically wonderful performance. And just after 1am, 'starry-eyed an' laughing as I recall' we headed off into the night. 'When's the next book coming out?' somebody asked me outside the venue. 'Soon,' was my reply. Except it hasn't been soon. It's taken its own time. Because we began again from the ground up: we put out more calls for writing, then came the selection process, the conversations, the editing, proofreading, artwork, typesetting, printing. . .and finally here it is.

The care with which we build these publications – never rushed, never to a deadline – is why I believe they'll continue to captivate people's minds. Well, that's the hope.

Once again, we collaborate with artists Lorna Robertson and Andrew Cranston. This time it's Lorna who provides the cover image, while Andy has created a sequence of new paintings specifically for this book. The cover is a brilliant departure in style from previous wurd covers. And we loved Andy's suggestion that – as most are of food – the images inside could be 'dispersed throughout like a little trail of snacks for the reader.' It's been a joy to work with these brilliant artists for a second time. I strongly recommend going to see their exhibitions if you get the chance, and definitely check out their recent publications of artwork:

thoughts, meals, days (2022) by Lorna Robertson and *Never a Joiner* (2023) by Andrew Cranston. I'm very grateful for the work they've put into this book.

In these pages, you'll find great pieces that will take you on journeys. So, I won't try to summarise, analyse or categorise. Personally, I'm looking forward to placing this volume next to *Alternating Current* on my bookshelf and taking a moment to think about all the writers and artists we've met and worked with to create around 500 pages of literary and visual art across these two books. Then it'll be on to the next project.

But let's pause for a moment. The combined force of *Alternating Current* and *Earthly Rewards* is a portrait of thi wurd, 2021-2024, and without hard work and an audience none of this would have happened. This comes with thanks to the team behind thi wurd, to the writers and artists, and to all the people who have supported us by buying books and magazines and attending events and classes.

And if you're reading this 60 years from now, well. . .I'm definitely not around, but I hope these pages still have the power to connect and draw people into stories, poems and art.

It's time for some earthly rewards.

Contents

Introduction – Alan McMunnigall	xi
Earthly Rewards – Joe Murphy	1
This world and all the pigeons that die in it – Holly Fleming	11
Strawheid – Gill Davies	14
:cartography of concepts IV – Diego Espíritu	17
Accidents & Emergencies – Debra Waters	21
Bonfires – Ian Farnes	33
The Lake Swimmer – Gerry Stewart	38
Lone Working – Gemma Elliott	40
The Sparrow – Chris Kinghorn	42
Eden – Eilidh Cameron	50
Sam Shepard – Eugene O'Hare	55

12th of July, 1992 – Eugene O'Hare	57
without (Extract) – Bechaela Walker	59
Dirt – Sarah Davy	67
Angels – Jerry Simcock	69
Holes – Joe Waite	75
Ashes to Ashes – Anjali Ramayya	78
Impressions – Anjali Ramayya	80
Batter (Extract) – Natalie Jayne Clark	81
Prince of Scars – Craig Johnson	86
Last Orders – Sophie Leslie	90
Wrang Words – Nicole Le Marie	92
The Parable of the Pangolin – Dom Howell	93
Case Study – Martin Geraghty	98
Disappearing – Sneha Subramanian Kanta	100
Dead End – Catriona Shine	102
Tight Lines – Mandy Watson	120
Reckoning – Regi Claire	122
MARK II – Caoimhín de Paor	125
What Casket – Tatora Mukushi	128
Quartet – Jon Russell Herring	132

For review/signature – Laura Givens	145
Meg's Day Off – Maggie Reeve	150
A Swear Jar for Saint Joseph – Matthew David Scott	154
[On a day] – David Harrison Horton	162
[Mid September's] – David Harrison Horton	163
Suffocation – Megha Shah	164
Pills 'n' Thrills and Bellyaches – Sean McMenemy	166
Don't feed the seagulls for they will end up knowing where you live – Kik Lodge	189
Just another day – Gillian Mayes	191
Arkansas – Carl Thompson	194
the x95 – Derek Murray	200
Exes – Ian Alexander	201
Concrete – Mel Piper	213
Working From Home – Simran Kaur	216
A Nice Guy – Wayne Dean-Richards	221
fifty first states (Extract) – Joanne Thomson	224
Three ways to travel – John G. Hall	230
The Exorcism of PTSD – John G. Hall	231
The Baths – Pamela McLean	233
Witness Protection – Kevin Cormack	242

List of Illustrations

By Andrew Cranston

Foosty plum	10
If you know your history	49
don't worry baby	66
Mirror phase	101
Half time	124
Proper way to draw figs	190
Painting makes nothing happen	215
Stands Scotland where it did?	223

Earthly Rewards

Joe Murphy

He was about ready for the off-licence when he heard knocking from somewhere inside the close. The paint scuttles were steeping in the bath – he'd managed to shower around them – and his sweat-soaked overalls lay in a heap in the corner. He'd got jeans and a t-shirt on, was struggling to get dry socks over still-damp feet. The knocking came again, accompanied by a voice.

He went into the hall, moved quietly down to the front door and put his eye to the spyhole. In round miniature he saw a woman dressed in black on her knees. She was holding his neighbour's letterbox open and shouting through. He looked up at the artex swirls of his ceiling, feeling what remained of the hangover coursing through his blood, then sighed and opened the door.

She was older – mid-fifties maybe – and when she glanced around he could see she was heavily made-up. Little chandeliers dangled from her ears. The close was heavy with the smell of her perfume. He watched her lift a brass knocker he had never noticed before and bring it down hard six times on the plate, each strike detonating off the walls.

Everything okay?

We were meant to be coming up here for a drink, but nobody's heard from her all day. She's not answering her phone.

She had the letterbox open again. When she leaned forward to bring her mouth to the gap her necklace of black stones clattered against the woodwork.

Out of charge maybe?

She dismissed this with a quick shake of her head.

Tracy, she shouted through the gap. Tracy, it's us. Are you there?

She's always on her phone, she said, straightening up. It's not just that, she's got this condition. Something with her brain. She's had scans but nobody knows what it is.

He realised he was still holding a sock and crouched to pull it on. He remembered finding Tracy two landings down, a while ago. She'd been sitting with both legs straight out in front, looking dazed, a spot of blood glistening below one nostril. It was a Friday night, so he'd assumed she was drunk. After they'd got her into her flat Moira had suggested phoning the hospital and he'd rolled his eyes.

She's just steamin, he'd said.

Listen, there's somebody coming with keys, said the woman. When they get here would you mind going in?

Her eyes were very wide. He could see the lines drawn along the edges, the mascara lying in clumps on the lashes. His headache was starting to ramp up.

I'll get my shoes.

On his way back out he heard voices, and glimpsed someone heading downstairs as he stepped onto the landing.

She'll be back up, said the woman.

He slotted in the larger key but it didn't need turning. When he turned the yale the door swung open. The light was on and the wide hall was bright and cheery, the floorboards a honey yellow with a big Persian rug down the centre. The space was still much cleaner looking than theirs. They had the same grubby carpet that was down when they moved in.

That's her bedroom, said the woman, her voice dropping to a whisper. First on the left.

Okay, he said, and stepped inside.

As he approached the door he saw it was fully closed. He reached out and gripped the handle. The woman had started whispering something over and over, very fast.

It was dark inside. He fumbled for the switch and snapped the light on. There was a double bed with the covers folded down tight, like in a hotel. A big mirrored wardrobe stood against one wall, an oval mirror draped in fairy lights on a stand in the corner; a chest of drawers beside that. On the bedside table was a framed photograph. It was her, a little younger, posing with a couple of friends. She looked good, smiling straight into the camera, dark hair chopped short around her shoulders, heavy-lidded green eyes as sexy as he remembered.

Nothing here, he said.

The woman's head appeared round the door.

Oh Jesus, she said. The bed's still made up.

They retreated, closing the door behind them.

When he started to cross the hall she touched his arm.

That's just a cupboard.

She pointed to the next door on this side.

That's the other bedroom.

As he moved towards it, it struck him that this room would be directly through the wall from their own, and so she must have used it as her main bedroom at some point. Strange that he'd never had a proper conversation with her, yet knew what she sounded like during sex. He and Moira used to hear her fighting with her ex-boyfriend, a Cockney, whose voice pierced easily through concrete and plaster when he was drunk. Which was often. Moira would talk about phoning the police, but he always stopped her. Different relationships had different rules, and besides, it was none of their business.

The door was open a foot or so. He got close to it. A wave of nausea passed through him and he waited for it to subside.

Please just do it, said the woman.

He pushed it all the way, wood scraping over carpet, then stepped in and switched the light on. Boxes were piled high against one wall, and an open suitcase lay on the single bed, clothes spilling from it over the duvet. From the hall he could hear the woman's shallow breathing. He went to the chest of drawers and slid the top one open. Inside rows of pants were folded into neat bundles. He loosened a green pair, rubbed the lacy edge between his thumb and forefinger. When a floorboard creaked he moved to the door and shook his head.

Nothing.

My God, said the woman, and brought her hand to her mouth. There was a sheen of sweat on her face. He touched a radiator and sure enough it was scalding.

What's this thing that's wrong with her?

She gets these blackouts.

And the doctors don't know what it is?

On the opposite side of the hall the toilet door stood open, the room empty.

That's the kitchen, she said, pointing to the last door on this side.

He stopped at the closed door and tried to gather himself. She was here. He was sure of it. Lying on the linoleum floor, surrounded by the smashed remains of whatever she had been reaching for – dried pasta, a glass jar in pieces, rice cascading over the counter and into her dark hair.

The handle was greasy with his sweat but he turned it and stepped through. Enough light was coming from the window to see by, rendering everything in a dull monochrome. It was a well-ordered space, very different from his own, the worktops devoid of any clutter – although something was lying there, out of place on the surface. He drew closer and saw it was a bottle opener, a good quality one with rectangular wooden panels on the handle. A cork was still attached to the screw. When he lifted it the smell of red wine made his stomach churn.

The woman said something, but her voice was barely audible. It sounded like she was trying to breathe through a tube. The room was calm and perfectly still. The clock on the wall had a gentle tick. He stood quietly, and watched the hand move slowly around the dial.

Is there something there?

No, he replied.

He found her standing with her back against the wall,

hands cupped over her mouth and nose. She was staring across the hall to the last door, where a light was flickering through the dark gap at the bottom.

It was only now, being this close, that they could see it. He heard the low murmur of voices, then applause and theme music from a quiz show.

He was next to her. Her eyes were open very wide and into his mind came the image of a dog straining desperately against its lead. The buttery smell of sweat lay under her perfume. He felt a twitch in his groin and imagined leaning in and kissing her hard on the mouth, putting his arms around her warm, trembling body.

He went forward and the woman came behind. He eased the door open.

She was lying on the rug, the flickering blue glow of the television playing over her skin, arms resting neatly across her chest as if she had been positioned that way. Her eyes were glazed and disturbingly dark, as though the pupils had swollen up, her mouth open just enough to show the bottom row of teeth, head tilted to the side to reveal the tip of the large tattoo that ran down her left side. She was wearing jogging bottoms, one slipper and a calfskin body warmer.

She's here, he said, I think she's gone.

When he stepped out, the woman was trying to dial a number on her phone, but her hands were shaking. She clutched the phone to her chest. C'mon Michelle, she said. Get it together. She looked at him sharply.

Did you check for a pulse?

He re-entered and crouched beside her. He tried not to look at her face and put his hand to her wrist. The skin was cool. In the strange light from the TV her face appeared a waxy yellow. He could not feel anything and knew that he should put his ear close to her mouth to listen for breath, but he had a terrible feeling if he did she would lurch up suddenly and clamp her teeth around his neck. He reeled on his haunches at the thought and almost overbalanced.

Voices were raised in the hall. There was a cry and a moment later the door was flung open and someone was shouting, Get away, get away from her, and then he was being pushed aside and this person fell onto the body, hugging it and beginning to sob. He rose and backed away.

The hall had filled with women, all dressed for a night on the town. Some were holding onto each other, some wiping away tears. He slipped past them and out onto the landing. John was just reaching the top of the stairs, banjo case in one hand, blue carrier bag in the other.

Alright man? We still on for tonight?

*

Once the story had been fully recounted and he'd steadied himself with one of John's cans, he decided to head to the off-licence. When he opened his front door, the women were there. They'd carried wooden chairs and placed them out on the landing and were now sitting straight-backed, nursing cups of tea. A couple of them smiled and said hello as he passed.

On his way back in with the beers a slim woman with glasses touched his arm and thanked him and he recognised her as the one who had shouted.

No problem, he said, and stopped. Listen, can I get yis a drink? A whisky or something?

Hands came up. They were fine with their tea. The woman who had been inside with him was seated at the centre. He tried to catch her eye, but she looked away.

*

The cop who came to his door later looked pale.

Carbon monoxide, he said. Were you in there for long?

Ten minutes maybe.

The guy nodded. Should be okay then. I would keep your windows open for a good while anyway. Sleep with them open if you can. It's all shut off now but there could be traces. If you start feeling sick then go get yourself checked out.

The guy wrote down his name, told him someone would be round the next day to take his statement.

Did you know her well, he said, as he was about to leave.

Couldn't have told you her first name before today.

The cop gave him a strange look, as if he was about to say something else, then nodded and turned away.

After John left he sat up alone, waiting for Moira to appear. He wanted to tell her the story, wanted to see the excitement building on her face as he spun it out. He was already reworking it.

Hold on, hold on, she'd tell him. Let me get a drink for this!

After a bit he went and looked through the spyhole, but the women were gone and the close was quiet. He took one of the German beers he'd been saving and brought it through to the living room. He knew what the cop had been about to say. Something about community or looking after your neighbours or how things were not the way they used to be.

He took the bottle opener out his pocket and turned it in his hands. The metal was a deep blue, and the finely polished grain of the panels caught the light; the hinge smooth from use. It was the kind of thing she might have kept as a memento from a bar job or a holiday somewhere. A reminder of some long-vanished event. He levered the cap off his beer with it, sat back, and waited.

This world and all the pigeons that die in it

Holly Fleming

We're on the motorway from town to Beith
on the first sunny day of 2021 and there is a maimed

pigeon in the back seat sliding around in a
printer box. This is the second time in a span of

twelve months that we have been in nearly this
exact situation. Ailing animals flock to his mother

like I don't know what. Last time it was a baby
seagull. This time it's a broken winged pigeon

in a printer box. We hear its wings flapping,
battling rescue. We're driving it into a sunset that it

cannot see. I think this is a very romantic notion
for a pigeon, but I have never thought of romantic notions

for pigeons before, so this could actually be
relatively tame. I think about holding its little wings

and raising it to the closed car window so it can watch the
sun fade away to twilight behind the treelines.

I think about comforting the little thing but I don't want
the diseases it may carry. The diseases it probably carries.

I try to speak to him but am often interrupted by the
sat nav's monotone. I cry

laughing when we imagine a car crash and our
deaths, we imagine paramedics tending to the pigeon

first and his mother, upon hearing about his death, asking,
"Did the pigeon make it?"

We rationalise the pigeon's way home by talking about its
homing ancestors. He imagines the pigeon as a

runaway dad. We drop it off at a house near a sign that reads
"Hedgehog Hospital." The drive home without the
   printer box and the

confused flapping of a broken wing against cardboard feels
lonely. We arrive home two hours later than usual having avoided

car crashes, and I am tired and I have forgotten much
   of this poem –

I tried to write it in my head, swore to myself I'd remember the words.

The gaps sound like confused flapping against cardboard.

Strawheid

Gill Davies

It was a scorching hot summer and I was on strike for most of it. Me and my pals would be on the picket line in the morning and we would come over to my bit in the afternoon. Sometimes we went to Viccy Park with a carry out. Strawheid and Old Jimmy were always there with their super lagers. I knew them from the Haggerston Estate where I was living at the time. It was on the council's 'hard to let' list. Strawheid was from Glasgow and Old Jimmy was from Dundee. Hackney was full of Scottish folk.

I had moved to London for work, they had moved to get away from stuff. They were great company. They gave my pals from Yorkshire a power, but it was all good-natured. Their patter was always flowing.

Someone told me Strawheid used to be a paratrooper and I thought they were at it. How the hell could he have been in the bloody army? This gentle soul with his long frizzy hair and his bellbottoms.

When I hadn't seen him on the estate for a while, I went to see his neighbour, Sheila. Everyone knew Strawheid never answered his door. She was just about to take him in his dinner and she said I could come in with her. There he was, sitting watching *Neighbours*. Sheila handed him his plate of mince and I asked him where he had been. He said he had been busy decorating. There was nothing in the room except the telly, a sideboard and a settee. There wasn't even a carpet on the floor.

I pointed at the photo on the wall, of a paratrooper jumping out a plane.

Is that you, Strawheid?

Aye.

He didn't elaborate.

Me and Sheila left so he could eat his dinner in peace. I asked her if she knew if it really was him in the photo.

Yeah, she said. He used to be in the Red Devils, you know.

Sheila told me he had been with the paras during the Troubles in Ireland. He had lost pals there and he had been in the Falklands too. When he came back, he went off the rails and they discharged him when he was caught with smack. To get off that, he had hit the bevvy.

When the strike finished and we went back to work, I got a new job. I started at eight in the morning, so I had to leave early bells. One day, I was on my bike going past the shop when I heard someone shouting on me. I looked back and there was Strawheid. I stopped and he walked over to me. I had never seen anyone shaking so much in my puff. He was carrying this can and he could hardly hold the bloody thing.

Gonnae help me hen, he said. I need a wee charge to

get me going. I took the can of super lager and opened it for him. It shoogled in his hands as he drank it. Couldn't get it down his neck quick enough.

:cartography of concepts IV

Diego Espíritu

confinamiento [lockdown]

resiliencia [resilience]

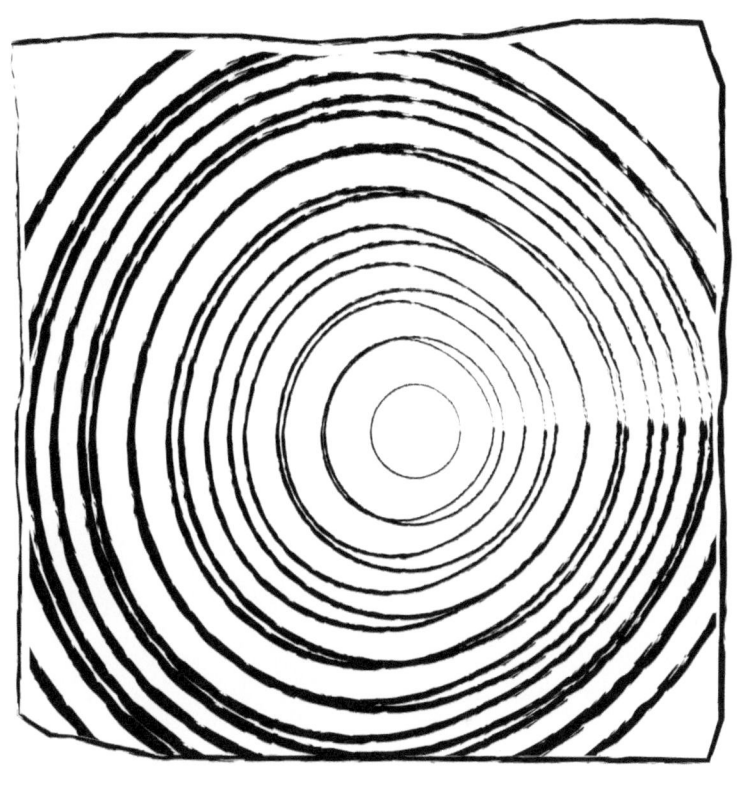

contención [containment]

pandemia [pandemic]

Accidents & Emergencies

Debra Waters

I'm no fan of Camberwell. When I lived there I was burgled, woke up to find a rat on my duvet, got spat at on the top deck of the No.36 bus, and pushed over for looking at someone's Big Mac. So I don't want to be at King's Hospital on a Wednesday night the week before Christmas.

A&E does a good job of patching up casualties before South London swallows them up again but it's plasters on open wounds. Tonight, there's a man with dementia covered in cuts, a tattooed woman crying and shouting and fist pumping the air, and a dozen people or more groaning or pressing on bloody makeshift bandages. A man with a ruby gash on his stubbly face is sat on a gurney being violently sick into a bucket; the odour infuses the hospital's antiseptic aroma with paprika and bile. I can cope with blood and shit and piss but vomit makes me cold-sweat-anxious.

My sister Lou is passed out on my left shoulder. Thin as paper since her divorce, her drunk weight is heavy and pulls on the tendons in my neck. Every few minutes her head falls forward so I push her gently back into the chair, study the rise and fall of her chest and listen to her slow, shallow breaths. Lou's pretty and looks younger than her age, but tonight her skin's pimpled and sore and her make-up's smeared. She's in her work clothes, a starched white shirt and tweed trousers, and the lapels of her smart taupe coat are lined with grime. Earlier, she'd received a poor performance review and dealt with it by drinking a bottle of Sauvignon Blanc and taking a handful of sleeping tablets she'd bought online.

*

I'd called her about our stepmother's Christmas present and heard her slurring.
'Hey, Lou, what's wrong?'
'Don't start, Little Blister.'
'Not starting. Are you OK?'
'Taken some pills, need to sleep.'
'How many pills?'
'A few.'
'How many?'
'Seven.'
'You only need one pill to sleep, Lou.'
'It was an accident.'
This isn't the first time my sister has been liberal with the recommended dosage. I tell her to unlock the front door and I call my doctor friend. She's at a work do in a Soho bar.
'What shall I do?' I'm knackered and want to watch *Diners, Drive-Ins and Dives* and eat oven chips.
'Take her to hospital. She might choke and she definitely

needs her blood pressure checked,' she says. In the background, her colleagues shout in agreement.

I get an Uber to Lou's house where I find her semi-conscious on the floor of her small, untidy kitchen. I crouch down and move strawberry blonde strands of hair from her face. Lou is the only fair-haired person in our family though we share the same blue eyes and ruddy cheeks. We used to tease her about it, telling her she'd been found on the steps of Durham Cathedral, but with her slight overbite and yo-yo moods there's no denying she's dad's flesh and blood. I pat her hand.

'Lou. Boo – Boozles, wake up.'

Lou smiles and starts to talk, her words the garbled language of someone lost to narcotics. I ask where her daughter is and she mumbles that she's with her dad. I check the bedrooms anyway then call another Uber, collect her bag and coat, and neck the remains of a glass of wine she's left on the laminate worktop.

'Silly girl,' I say in the cab, because I never think to call my middle-aged sister a woman.

'Love you, Little Blister,' she murmurs.

9.30pm

I half-carry, half-walk Lou into the hospital. In a font as benign as a Spanish hotel's the sign above the door says:

Reception Resuscitation

It could just as easily read 'Restaurant Pool'. A navy-clad nurse walks by carrying yellow plastic cases in each hand. 'Looking for A&E?' she says. 'Left through those doors.' We

23

check in and are seen quickly. A nurse with a Derry accent takes a vial of Lou's blood, checks her blood pressure, and sends us back to the triage area. The blood tests will take a few hours so we have a wait ahead. If all she needs is to sleep it off I can take her home, I suggest. I look at Lou – she's as peaceful as a babe in arms. I'm now concerned I'm wasting NHS resources and, knowing what triggers my own melancholy, dreading a night with no sleep. No, says the nurse. Stay.

It's for the best. If I took Lou to my house her despair might sully the cheery Christmas ambience. I've always believed sorrow can permeate walls and, like asbestos, pollute the people who live there. So, I sit and watch her sleep. I love my sister but I'm exhausted by her highs and lows, and mistrustful of her affections, which so quickly morph into accusations. While people dream of being free to travel or change careers, I fantasise about being free from her.

10.30pm
Lou is still passed out and the Wi-Fi is patchy so I talk to the people sitting near us. I've lived in London too long to speak to strangers but A&E has a perverted festive feel.

'What's wrong with her?' asks Enrico. Enrico's from a town near Madrid. He works in hospitality.

'She's taken too many pills.'
'On purpose?'
'Kind of. What about you, are you ok?'
'Yeah,' he says. 'Same old.'

Marcel's got cerebral palsy. He's tall and friendly and wears designer trainers. He asks after Lou.

'Why is she unhappy?'

'A few reasons.'

'Poor lady.'

Diane's from Peckham. She's got a pain in her side. She finishes an egg then asks around for food. I give her a squashed Twix from the bottom of my bag. The vomiting man continues to retch so I bury my nose in my sister's hair – it smells of her perfume, of violets and vanilla. The others gape at the man like he's a sideshow act and when a porter brings an empty bucket Enrico lets out a cheer.

As a distraction I play a game of A&E bingo in my head: *blanket toilet pain gurney doctor nurse hurts drugs wait soon calm down please.*

11.30pm

A friend texts and I send back a flare: *At a n e, sis overdose.* She calls but I don't pick up – it's hard to hear over the groaning and chatting and swing doors slamming. Waves of staff in kelp green and deep blue ebb and flow through the department. Sometimes the place is awash with them; other times, when they're occupied in curtained cubicles and I'm left alone with the walking wounded, the atmosphere reminds me of a horror film.

Midnight

A nurse with wide-set eyes checks Lou's blood pressure. 'Low but stable,' she says. Lou breaks into a goofy smile and collapses onto my shoulder. I envy her lying there, sleeping soundly. Jesus, I'm jealous of a woman who overdosed. I pinch my arm as punishment. 'Will we see a doctor soon?' I ask, meaning how soon can we leave. I don't have the guts for A&E.

'Soon, soon,' the nurse says.

1am

I'm tired and bored and need a wee. I check Lou's bag for dregs of coke; it's the party season so there might be some in her purse. I've warned her about self-medicating but the truth is we're as bad as each other. I find some and justify taking it because I need to be awake but numb. It's what we do, take little amounts, almost placebo. Tiny toots she calls them, enough to suppress the seesaws in our brains – even if the next day our moods are more extreme.

Enrico's left and Marcel's being seen so Diane says she'll keep an eye on Lou who's now asleep on a row of chairs and covered with my coat. Diane's reading a battered copy of *The Sun* and eating a packet of custard creams, having rejected an onion bhaji. 'No offence,' she says to the elderly Indian woman, 'but my stomach can't take the spices.' I pop a bhaji in my mouth and thank her with my mouth full. Then I grab Lou's purse and my bag.

On my way back, I pass the resuscitation ward. The doors open and I see where the real shit is happening. A male nurse speed walks past with a portable defibrillator, a disembodied voice shouts for adrenaline. There's a woman my age being moved away from a bed, clenched fists to her mouth. The doors shut and I stand there for a few seconds, ashamed, hating myself and the coke's acrid taste at the back of my throat, fearful of what it's doing to my heart.

Back at A&E things are quieter; apart from the odd whimper, people are sleeping or stooped over their phones playing *Candy Crush*.

1.45am
A nurse with a grey pixie cut takes Lou's blood pressure and asks if Lou's been sick. I shake my head. I want to make conversation, ask her where she's from, but she's in no mood for small talk. 'Are we close to seeing a doctor?' I ask. 'Soon,' she says.

2am
Lou's asleep on my lap, curled up like a fern. I watch a paramedic move a curly-haired teenager from a stretcher to a gurney. I always thought ambulance staff dropped off patients and headed straight out, but the paramedic has her hand on the boy's forehead and she's soothing him. 'I'm not going anywhere,' she says, with a warmth that makes me want to hug her – or, better still, be hugged by her. He's wearing pyjama bottoms – no top – and there are bandages on his wrists. There's not much blood so I hope it's not serious, except of course it is because he felt desperate enough to do it. Just a flesh wound, I think, like Monty Python's Black Knight. 'Tis but a scratch, I hope.

I only needed an ambulance once, when I was 17. Mum had died in the winter and by summer dad's healing process entailed a period of unbridled promiscuity followed by a Prozac overdose. Lou was away, studying. One Christmas – the first without mum – dad threw our undercooked turkey across the kitchen, cursed us kids for existing, and we went to our separate bedrooms to watch TV. That's when I got a taste for the anaesthetising effect of alcohol.

The following July was my turn – depressed and grieving, I overdosed and was rushed to York Hospital where I had my stomach pumped. Afterwards, I was placed on a ward with three old ladies who, between sharing copies of *Take a Break* and *Good Housekeeping*, kept themselves busy by knitting and slagging me off:

'Selfish madam. Hardly an emergency when there are people with real problems.'

'She should try living with bladder cancer.'

'What must her mother think?'

I hid under the blankets sweating and repeating over and over, 'Fuck you, fuck you, you dried-up bunch of bitches.' But they did me a favour – my anger made me realise I wasn't as numb as I thought.

2.30am

Lou stirs; she needs the toilet. We walk unsteadily to the bathroom and as I help her undress I notice she's had an accident. This happened to mum when we couldn't get her out of her wheelchair in time, and it happens to me since I gave birth. It's a private stigma, a reminder of how our bodies fail us.

When we get back an officer is attending to a bleeding homeless man with missing teeth and rough patches on his scalp. He tells a joke and the policeman laughs, genuinely laughs, at the punchline. The policeman's left hand is on the man's back and he keeps it there, even after their conversation trails away, only removing it when a nurse comes over.

I realise that although I've broken rules in furtive ways – doing 30 in a 20 zone, taking drugs in club toilets – I'm terrified of the captivity that comes from breaking the law.

3.15am
We are guided into a cubicle. A young male nurse does more checks – blood pressure, temperature. Lou's blood tests have come back; no problems there. Lou's drowsy but awake. She's given a glass of cold water and asked more health questions. The nurse is attentive and non-judgmental, and I feel a guilty creep of longing for his empathy.

The nurse leaves. Lou looks around and reads out the words on a sexual health poster, 'Your condom or mine'. She looks at me quizzically and curls a lip like Elvis. 'That doesn't even make sense.' She starts to laugh and I join in. This is why I carry her, for these moments when we're aligned by a shared hilarity for the absurdities of life – a badly written public health poster, pornographic clouds, men in whitewashed denim.

We laugh until we cry. I catch my breath and say, 'Do you remember how, every time we had a laughing fit, mum would say "it'll end in tears"? It made me think even good things have to end badly.'

'No wonder we're such fuck-ups.'

'Speak for yourself.'

I stroke some strands of hair from Lou's face and tuck it behind her left ear.

'Look how far we've come,' I say. It's meant to be ironic but we have. We've endured deaths and breakdowns, we've made lives for ourselves, yet it always feels like catastrophe is looming.

3.45am
Gupta, the mental health nurse, arrives and asks Lou if she's done anything like this before. She has, a few times, since she was 13.
'No.'
After assurances that Lou's daughter is at her dad's, and that Lou will call her therapist and see the GP about increasing her dose of antidepressants, she's signed off on the agreement that I'll keep an eye on her.

4.30am
I order a cab. I have that empty feeling you get when you're dog-tired and hungry. The last time I was up this late I was in labour, in the same hospital. It's still dark but birds are singing. We stand outside A&E on Denmark Hill, opposite the Maudsley Psychiatric Hospital.
'Didn't you spend a week there?' says Lou.
'Nah, it was only a night.'
She looks at me. 'You were there a few days, Blister. I remember because it was just before the solar eclipse. You kind of lost it after you left that weird theatre group – didn't the director try to get you all to sleep with each other in the name of art?'
I was 24 and as ill as Lou is now. It was after my second – and final – overdose. How did I get stronger, while my

sister still struggles?' 'I don't really remember,' I say. Lou links her arm through mine and squeezes it.

'Camberwell sucks,' she says.

4.45am
We get into a cab and are lulled by the warmth and movement of the Prius. Heart FM's playing Phyllis Nelson's 'Move Closer'. I slow-danced to it at a school disco when I was 12, with a black-haired boy called Dom. It was awkward and lovely. I was excited about growing up. Soon after that Lou was admitted to a psych ward.

Lou's looking out of the window. I put my hand on her leg and she turns to me, glassy-eyed.

'Do you remember having family therapy on the psych ward?' I say. It's not the right time to mention it but I ask because going to therapy together was the last time I remember us being an unbroken family.

Lou grins. 'Dad got me through that.'

'Daddy's girl,' I say, smiling.

'It's not that, he understood. I was on that ward with girls way worse off than me; one of them was raped by her granddad for fuck's sake. There was nothing wrong with me compared to them.'

'You weren't well, Lou.'

'The doctors said it was puberty hormones.' She looks down and starts to pick at the skin around her Shellac nails.

'Well, something sparked your breakdown.'

'Dad said it was in our family, in our blood.'

She looks at me and I can see, then, how scared she is

of being lonely, how she's going to spend the rest of her life doing anything not to feel alone.

I lie back on the leather seat. I'm craving bagels.

'Thanks, Little Blister.'

'For what?'

'You know what.'

'No problem, Boozles.'

'You know,' she says, 'I really appreciate what you did tonight but taking me to hospital? I think you overreacted a bit,' and she rests her head on my shoulder and goes back to sleep.

Bonfires

Ian Farnes

I've gone past this house wi my wee boy every day this week and I've no seen anyone. Look around the hedge: no-one. You see the grass cut short, red roses, tulips through, like wee balloons on sticks, just like you get in aw the gardens on this street.

A cul-de-sac and hardly the arse end, every house
   a garden, back and front.
The path, the four steps up, the door.

I couldni mind, him or his family. That they'd
   even stayed there.
Different times, all over
done wi.

Now I dinni ken if they're in there, or no in there, or what and it's no like his family belongs the town

they didni. . .

and they wereni. . .

Dan, his name was.
Danny.
Danny's house.

He coulda lost an eye, we watched it happen,
me and aw the boys I kicked about the town wi.

Wouldni say we were a gang
the four of us
but gangs of girls would hang around wi us
and odd relationships might start, at parties.

Aw that energy: Craig's bedroom door was
full of holes. His bedroom wall.
The biggest hole hid by a poster that said
Kill 'Em All.

The party when Craig's folks were out of town;
wi aw the boys from up The Castle in the street
we left them out there.
Left them all outside.
One boy chucked a stone
and that was that.

      Boundaries crossed, and where to draw the line.

The school bus. Top deck, back end, Danny got himsel
   the wrong side
punched some wee guy in the face:

big rugby boy he was
he punched this wee boy
backa the heid,
eight or nine times
wee boy hid his face
behind his arms

    Danny's parents let their hedge
    grow big. It takes up half the path.

    I dinni ken who Danny's dad is
    what he looks like now.
    He could come out his house
    and walk right past
    a wee nod.
    up the road. Like,
    who am I to him?
    A nothing.

    Not a single word would pass between us.

The four of us stood watching.
Aw the toun out for the fire and the fireworks
Aw the gadgies, husbands, wives aw bairned up,
out for bonfire night.

    A bone-fire. That's the thing it's from
    A bone-fire
    not from *bon* from French,

    not likes as if to say a *good* fire
    but *bones burned in a fire*

    bones of people, witches and the like:
    those outside what is,
    or was accepted
    not the effigies
    but the hings theresels.

We all stood watching.

Danny wasn't one of us. A big boy for his age.
A good home. Aw that confidence.
They took turns kicking his head,
his eye, one of his eyes, swelled up like a baseball,
like a fuckin cricket ball.

The fireworks almost done, they jumped him, three or four boys all at once to bring him down and his legs went, then one boy rushed in, kicked big Danny in the head, then ran back and another boy would rush in, kick him, two or three times, run back in the crowd.

    I can't believe you never helped him. Danny's Dad said after.

    So,
    that's his house,
    the wee one sleeping in the buggy;

I'm stood at the threshold, daft.
There's been too much of this shite,
ever since my boy was born:
thinking of what others felt,
or might be feeling
still.

There has to be a limit.

A rugby-playing kid from a house
with a huge fucking hedge.

Don't even think about it.

The Lake Swimmer

Gerry Stewart

for Saara

She is a feather suspended
in the mirror face,

a water skater
denting the surface of clouds.

An unbroken wavering.

Her arms rainbow to the sky.

Each stroke opens the depths,
opens her.

A dive warms like a hint of sun
before the storm.

The rain, the lake, the swimmer,
one in reflection.

The weathered board ladder
is the anchor,
she sails without desire of return.

Lone Working

Gemma Elliott

When the gallery closes you're the only one asked to stay. Your manager is ever so polite about it: would you, could you, do you mind? The insurance needs someone to keep the lights on until we can sell.

It's a relief at first to get away from the questions and complaints of the public. Not to have to find another job quite yet. You have the place to yourself, a little kitchenette, something to read, the quiet.

You find it easy to slip into talking to yourself. First, the odd emotive slip. An article or opinion you don't approve of. Aye right. Come on. Cunt. Those don't need a response, so you barely notice that there's no one around to agree or otherwise. Your colleagues hadn't always replied anyway. But the longer you work alone, the more that needs to be said. You have to remember how to speak and how to listen.

Narrating each day becomes a way to cope with the isolation and the boredom, to make your existence more real. Like there's a pet at your feet you say, let's have some lunch shall we, time for a walk round Gallery A to stretch the old legs. This progresses into you taking the starring role in the documentary of your life, playing both subject and narrator. At eleven each day the human worker pauses, rises, and flicks on the kettle. Only time will tell if today is a day for coffee or a day for tea.

With very little to do, it comes as no surprise that you slip into conversation with yourself eventually. When your manager shows up to let you go, you're involved in a fierce debate over what painting used to hang opposite your favourite invigilator's chair. You think it was 1950s abstract expressionism. You think it was something like a Constable. Your manager interrupts to remind you it had been a photography exhibition and to ask you, please, to leave.

The Sparrow

Chris Kinghorn

I stared out the window of the taxi as the towering motorway lights gave way to busy streets and tightly packed tenements. These were soon replaced by the sparse streets of north Glasgow, grey houses to the left, a row of run-down shops with just a bookies and off-licence at the other side. I couldn't even look at Ed as the driver took a sharp left into the housing scheme leaving the amber glow of the main road behind. I could feel his growing excitement as the car climbed the hill too quickly for comfort — why did private cabs always go so fast?

Then we stopped. The driver said nothing, a man of few words who didn't even question why a wee posh boy from the southside and a Yank would have any business in The Sparrow. I kept my arms folded and let Ed square up the driver, the least he could do.

We got out and the taxi did a quick birl in the road and sped away like he was fleeing the scene of a crime. The Sparrow stood before us: a windowless, grey lump of concrete that looked like it belonged in Soviet Crimea. Ed grinned and held his hand out for me to lead the way. Aye right.

I followed him in. A narrow foyer led onto the main bar. I dug my fingernails into my palms as Ed pushed open the door and strolled through — no going back now. I could feel every eye in the place on us. We were by far the youngest people there. It was pretty quiet, which I took as a good sign. Three middle-aged guys held up the bar to our right and a few of the tables were occupied. Ed swaggered straight up to the bar. The cockiness of Americans never ceases to amaze me. Or was it a basic lack of self-awareness?

The barmaid looked unimpressed as he ordered our usual in that loud Yank accent: a pint of Guinness for him and Tennent's for me. This got the attention of the boys at the bar right away.

— Awright, lads? Yous American?

— Yeah, Ed chirped. — From Philly.

— Aw nice, mate. Av goat an uncle ower there. Near Boston he is am sure.

— Oh yeah? Sweet.

— Tony here used tae work in the States anaw, didn't ye, Tone?

— Aye. Worked in the oil fields up in Alaska, the boy growled. — Froze ma fuckin baws off every day of the week for about seven year. Good money but. He grinned and took a slug of his pint.

— What brings yees up here?

— I hate the city centre bars, Ed replied without missing a beat. —They're all soulless as shit.

— Fair play mucker and what about yerself? You American anaw?

I felt my cheeks flush instantly as his eyes turned on me.

— Naw, I'm southside, I said, trying to be as vague as possible.

— Aw aye. Long way from home up here, eh?

He turned to the bar.

— Same again, Nancy hen. Well enjoy yer night, lads. Anyone gies ye any hassle just tell them yer pals wi Big Eric. He gave us a wink then turned away. Ed looked at his Guinness that had been set down on the bar in a Foster's glass, a big white head almost halfway down the glass.

— Leave it, I said.

I found us a corner seat that was close to the door with our backs to the wall. I felt calmer now we'd sat down and were away from Big Eric's spotlight. Ed had been slightly economical with the truth in his explanation, although it was true in part. The reason we were there was because one night in the student bar I had drunkenly agreed to find a list of the five roughest pubs in Glasgow and take him to them. Over the last few weeks I'd been to parts of the city I never even knew existed but this was the one I was most worried about.

Since we'd sat down, a steady stream of new punters had been making their way into the bar. I took a nervous sip of my pint. All it took was someone that didn't like your face in these places. I'd heard enough stories from my old man. Ed was looking pretty chuffed with himself.

— Wanna game of pool?

— No chance, I said, noticing the table across from us, commanded by two guys in their thirties.

— You're such a pussy, man.

— You can't just go up for a fucking game, I hissed

— You need to beat one of those guys to even get a shot. It's a fucking lose-lose situation.

I took another slurp of my pint. The sooner we could go the better.

— Are yees in for the dominoes the night, boys? A woman had appeared at Ed's shoulder.

— Ummm. . .

— Fiver entry. Winner gets fifty quid and a hamper.

Ed was nodding already. — Sounds awesome.

So half an hour later I found myself around a big cluster of tables that we'd helped join together. The lights had been brought up slightly so you could see every crease and scar on your opponent's face. There were ten of us playing, mostly older guys that had made a special appearance for the dominoes it seemed. It was a first to ten games scenario, winner takes all. I hadn't played since my holidays in the Algarve as a wee boy so I wasn't particularly worried. Ed on the other hand revealed himself to be a bit of a dominoes shark. Within an hour and a half, he was level at nine points each with this dour-looking baldy boy. He clearly wasn't used to being rattled on his own turf by a cocky young American. I held my breath and prayed for Ed to chap the table in resignation but he kept placing the tiles down in that slow dramatic style I could only assume was tactical. I glanced round the table. Every eye was fixed on the game, no one dared look away. Big Eric and his mates at the bar had stopped chatting to watch. I looked over at the door. We'd be away after this anyway, just sit tight for another few minutes, I told myself. I turned back round and the baldy boy looked down at his hand slowly then rapped the table. Chapping. Ed followed on with his double three and he was out. He'd won the game, the money, the hamper. But he'd stolen this guy's pride in his own local and I was more than a tad apprehensive about how he would react. He rose from his seat, however, and extended his hand to Ed.

— Well played, young man.

— Thanks. Ed grabbed his hand and shook it, that big friendly labrador beam spreading across his face as everyone began to applaud.

— Right, I'm going for a piss then phoning us a taxi, I said, as Ed was led up to collect his prize.

I went through the door that had a big head-shaped indentation and into the gents. I puffed out my cheeks, letting out a long exhale as I stared at the ceiling and began to piss. That hadn't actually gone too badly, I considered, but it was time to make tracks. As I went to wash my hands I looked at my face in the cracked mirror and allowed myself a chuckle. The Sparrow was the last pub on our list; thank fuck that bet was over. I never wanted to have a pint outside of Sauchiehall Street for the foreseeable. Next second, I heard a massive whoop followed by a mix of baying cheers and jeers.

— Who the fuck put that oan?

I left the toilet and the opening pulse of the Rangers anthem 'Simply the Best' by Tina Turner filled my ears. Ed was up in the middle of the floor dancing with the dominoes woman. She was lost in his eyes, grinding up against his leg as he fist-pumped the air. It occurred to me right then that I hadn't even considered the affiliations of this bar. They usually consisted of the biggest psychos from both sets of Glasgow fans. I scanned the faces. Half the dominoes team were whooping in encouragement as Ed dirty danced with Dominoes Lady, another few looked as if they were ready to lob their pints at him.

— Get this tae fuck! A shout came from the far corner.

I'd managed to avoid fighting my whole life — something of a minor miracle as I was both specky and ginger — and I had no intention of starting now.

The baldy guy from the dominoes appeared at Ed's shoulder, patting him on the back and handing him a fresh pint. Brilliant. The cheers and heckles escalated before the song was eventually skipped by Nancy behind the bar. Groans of disappointment and shouts of appreciation.

— Yer pal nearly caused a rammy there, Baldy chuckled, thrusting a Tennent's into my hand.

— You didn't have to! I shouted as he disappeared into the toilet.

I sat back down at our corner table and took a gulp of beer as 'Kingston Town' came on and the whole place melted into one again. The lager was starting to chill me out a bit and I felt a mellow glow wash over me. The dance floor was filling up now, Ed at the centre laughing his head off. I started to laugh too and took my phone out to get a picture of him in his element.

As Nancy shouted for last orders, Ed insisted on buying everyone a drink with his winnings. Who was I to argue with him? Then everyone was trying to down their halves, there were shouts to drink up and get moving, people were pulling on their coats and spilling out onto the street. I had to drag Ed away from Dominoes Lady as we made for the taxi.

— Yous be back the morra for the karaoke, aye?

— Sure we will!

I grabbed his hamper, opened the door and shoved him in.

His head lolled back on the headrest as the taxi spun away from The Sparrow and he laughed again. Why could Americans not handle their bevvy?

— Seriously dude, I'm going back there tomorrow!

— Are you fuck, I said, lifting the lid of the hamper for a wee nosy.

DAVID HOCKNEY

Mr. and Mrs. Clark and Percy 1970-1

Eden

Eilidh Cameron

26 July

I feel her fingers inside me. I close my eyes, bum tensing, back inching away from the bed. My knees quiver slightly, toes curling into each corner. *Try to relax.*
 'So, do you live local?'
 She digs, and the speculum prises me open. Poking, pinching, cramping. It's far up, right below my abdomen, a spot I've never felt before. I find myself speaking to the doctor. One final tug, and then release, like the ping of an elastic band.
 'Well done Eden, that's you. Sit up slowly now, you might feel a wee bit dizzy at first.'
 I rise, and feign a smile.
 'That's great, thanks. Way quicker than I thought.'
 As soon as I speak, I feel a wave of nausea, and my eyes blur.
 'I'll get you a glass of water. Take your time, and pop off the bed when you're ready, then we can have a quick chat. There might be some bleeding, I've left you a sanitary towel on the chair there.'
 She swings the paper sheet round its rail to give me some

privacy, and I down the cup of water, teeth scraping against the plastic rim. A few deep breaths, and I feel slightly better. I do my best to 'pop' off the bed. I'm not sure where to put the scratchy cover-up she gave me, so I fold it as neatly as I can and put it on the chair.

*

I breeze out of the building, past the lines of women waiting for their turn. Someone has replaced me on the hospital bed. It feels good to stretch my legs, to bring life back into them and steady the shakes. I navigate through the car park and wait to cross the road, as I feel the first murmurings inside me. Murmurings turn into jolts, and then searing pain twists around my stomach, splintering down my back. I breathe in and start walking as the green man flashes.

It takes all my strength not to go straight into the flat. Instead, I grab the essentials from the shop downstairs. Lucozade. Ibuprofen. Paracetamol. Go to the self-checkout so I don't have to speak to anyone. Up the stairs, shove my key into the lock. Dump everything on the kitchen table and stick the kettle on. Go through to our room and change straight into comfy clothes, bringing my hot water bottle back through. Swallow painkillers, grab the Lucozade and get into bed.

I put on the TV and try to relax through the pain, but the flickering picture makes me feel worse. I shut my eyes, hot water bottle pressed against my groin, and curl up. Foetal position.

*

I stir from my half-sleep and wait for the pain to return. It does, duller than before, but the nausea seems to have passed. I mash the buttons on my phone to check the time before taking more painkillers. It's two o'clock. Ally will be back around six, so I have time to pull myself together.

12 July

He slurps noisily from his cereal bowl. Coco Pop-stained milk drips onto the white sleeves of his crisply ironed shirt, the remnants congealing at the corners of his mouth. I look away.

The radio cuts through the silence in the room, its theme urgent and familiar.

'Good morning, and welcome to BBC Radio Scotland. Today we're hearing from our environment correspondent, Ruth, who's asking: would you give up having children in order to save the planet?'

I pause, teaspoon touching the golden yolk of my boiled egg. The noise sucks me in: a series of interviews with experts and then members of the public phoning in as the voice of reason. I scoop out the insides and swallow as I listen, dissatisfied. I'd taken the egg out of the boiling water one minute too soon, leaving its insides watery. I remind myself I should probably go vegan.

'Eden, my love, have a good day. Don't work too hard.'

He kisses my cheek from behind, then clatters his bowl into the sink. Hot coffee breath lingers around my face. I was too intent on listening to notice him.

27 July

'Are you alright, Eden? You're a bit pale.'

His kindness is suffocating, and I bite back.

'Period pains, that's all.'

'Oh. . .I see.' He looks crestfallen. 'I'll run you a bath?'

'Thanks, Ally.' I smile, softening for a moment before the guilt rises.

It's Saturday, and there's a heatwave brewing, with record temperatures expected. I sit on the window seat, legs stretched out, window wide open. The sun bathes me gently, not yet blazing. These used to be our favourite kind of days – no plans, no weddings, no baby showers. Maybe we'd have a lie in, read the papers in bed together. Maybe we'd walk to the local bakery, pick up some nice bread and wine, maybe we'd take it to the park and drink it in the afternoon sun, getting quietly tipsy and talking through our weeks. Maybe.

I have an article to write up for work, which I'll do after my bath. The gym is out of the question, cramps still haunting me, and so the day stretches out, empty.

*

I step in slowly, toes tingling with the shock. Knees, thighs and back. Ally knows how I like my baths, on the verge of too hot so I can add the cold once I'm in there. I submerge myself, bubbles crowding around, and the heavy scent makes me drowsy. I touch the taps with my feet, savouring the icy drips, and wishing I'd brought a glass of water with me. My face begins to flush.

The door handle clicks and Ally appears, cup of coffee in hand and golden hair sticking up as he holds the door open.

'Let's go out for lunch. My treat.' He beams.

I heave myself up, gripping the handles on the side of the bath.

'I've got quite a lot to do today.'

'Come on, you've been working all week. We could go to that new place in Finnieston?'

The thought of strolling around Finnieston on a Saturday distracts me. Beanie hats and pushchairs, dungarees and students. I do want to try that restaurant. Mediterranean small plates and natural wine, it's been featured in several 'must-try' lists in the weekend supplement. Something Ally has obviously kept up his sleeve.

I surrender. 'Sounds good.'

He smiles, mid-sip, eyes widening.

'I'll phone and book a table. Enjoy your bath.'

He turns to leave and I slide under the water, thinking about the article that needs written. My abdomen crackles.

Sam Shepard

Eugene O'Hare

your final book- trailing death-
Spy of the First Person
takes no rest in short pages-

in every chapter i could hear something
being mauled close by in the yard.

the dead chicken knew way before
that wire fence is a man-made mirage–

stretched archly from post to post–
a telegraphed order, yet no more fixed
than the behaviour of the past; thriving
in deranged misremembrances;
double-measured, specimen-glassed.

i've been awake since five awaiting
the first rattling sounds of day to distract
itself from a desire to begin by screaming.

i cannot tell if the houseplant on this table
is alive/dead. more certain is the moving

footage in my head of all the dogs you owned
returning for an hour to observe your body;

the legs brushed, the hands that fed,
washed, held, leashed and freed,
and the mouth- quiet now
with no command to heed.

12th of July, 1992

Eugene O'Hare

with the town half closed,
we made a movie theatre
in the living-room.

curtains dragged together
like two shy boys forced to hug,
five of us with feet up,
bowls of Tayto, jars of mineral
from the Sodastream,
& Ma upstairs
cleaning out her wardrobes
for Saint Vincent de Paul.

Lethal Weapon, Raid on Entebbe,
Problem Child, Jaws.
we rewatched them all.

the day passed outside.
we turned up the volume to cover
the occasional bleed of a fire engine,

& distant drums belted down some road
we couldn't care a fuck about,
& flutes our dog mistook for whistles.

that night, uncle Jim come round
for a few cans and a bit of craic—

the pope and two orangemen
walk into a bar. . .

without (Extract)

Bechaela Walker

Half her life was spent at bus stops. They can put a man on the moon, but there's no real impetus to transport citizens from one part of a city to another in any sensible fashion. And it was almost a fiver now, not far off London prices, no return tickets either: only a single or a day. Why were things arranged in this manner, against the interests of the vast majority of human beings? She wedged her bag between her legs and struggled out of her jumper, pushing up the long sleeves of her thermal top. It was close, as if the puddles were evaporating. It had looked cold this morning, but the weather. You never could tell. Even now, if she looked in one direction, it was deep blue sky with little wisps of white clouds, but look westwards and it was a storm coming, almost black, and then the ferns all down the embankment, the foxgloves out, the buttercups bright and glowing in the gloom. The whole place smelled of coconut from the gorse, like suntan oil, and it always made her think of sex. She thought of John, the argument they'd had that morning, and wanted to lie down there and then in the long grass, just fall down onto the earth, feel it damp beneath her, fluffy seeds floating through the air.

But there was work, and it wasn't the place to do such a thing — she'd look mad by the roadside, just lying there. All these unspoken rules though, how there's so few places you're permitted to rest, never mind lie down — whole pedestrian precincts designed to deter the very act of sitting, while in other countries it's socially acceptable to stop and relax, maybe even converse with others who are doing the very same thing.

She needed a pee too, but that was another conundrum: no public toilets, and yet everybody, everybody — it was a natural function for god's sake. The 12:15 definitely hadn't come, because she'd been more than five minutes early, and the next one wasn't due for another 35 minutes. She waded through the ferns at the back of the stop and over a rusted barbed-wire fence that had been trampled into the ground, coming out onto the towpath and starting along it towards the town. Why did she always have to walk so fast? She didn't have to be back at the office for any particular reason, and nobody knew where she was, nobody cared. But she had this invisible boss in her head who watched her every move. It was pathetic. She wrangled her phone out of her bag to catch up with some calls as she walked but the battery was at 1%. She upped her pace, deciding for sure to walk the whole way rather than chancing it with a bus. What was so urgent that she needed to push herself like this? Check her emails, make some calls: nothing urgent, nothing life-threatening. But she always felt ready to be found out. It was the same with friendships: pure worry. That's why she kept doing these stupid work courses, why she said yes to everything and ended up too tired to do her own stuff.

Something darted across the path. Not a mouse, not a rat; more like a fat little guinea pig, but fluffier, and reddish-brown. She typed in 'canal mammal red' but the phone shut down. Where had it gone? The sun beat through the thin leaves, filtering the light so that the air took on the quality of gauze, and each fluffy seed and insect, every bumble bee and butterfly seemed suspended in time. She needed this: to be out with no phone, no purpose, just being. She dropped her bag and pushed through the undergrowth, dropping her trousers and squatting behind a broad tree trunk. It felt so good. She watched the urine pool between her boots. There was a condom packet stuck into a slit of bark that peeled away from the trunk, some empty energy drink cans, balloons, and a cache of about fifty tiny silver pellets.

The tarry earth was speckled with star-shaped flowers from the tree above, like confetti. A deep gust of warmish air moved through the bushes and the trees. A pigeon cooed. She made the same noise back and it replied. She shook herself, bounced on her haunches and whipped up her trousers, rubbing her pants against the wet to dry herself.

Why hadn't she gone earlier? She was always holding things in, unable to access the stuff she wanted to, the emotional parts. She wasn't trying to keep it in, it was just locked in there.

Christ, why couldn't she use this time to compose a story in her head, to think of a good idea or to plan something nice? It was just endless drivel. She tried to force herself to be in the moment again: the sun sparkling on the canal, the lilies dotted along the water, a bush with tiny purple flowers that the bees obviously favoured. In fact, the more you looked at this bush, the more you realised it was literally covered with bees, to the point where it looked like it was moving, like the plant itself was an animal. Her throat contracted.

It would be good to get rid of the bag, just walk along the canal unencumbered. She rolled back her shoulders and tried to take deep breaths of air. Breathing like that, it sometimes made matters worse, making you aware of the fact you couldn't breathe. But that was ridiculous, you were breathing all the time, so it was best to just let it happen and not start up with the big deep hippy breaths at all, just breathe and be done with it. Christ almighty, the self-improvement, would it ever stop. She'd been wanting to take Finn along here on his bike, but she'd had a nightmare of him going into the water and her being unable to get him out because in this nightmare, the water was deep as a loch and he just sank and sank. Realistically, it couldn't be that deep, because there was a Portaloo sticking out the water, so it must only be about chest-high, except at the locks. This book she was reading advised challenging your catastrophic thinking with facts, and here was the fact before her, proving that if he fell in, the worst he'd get was wet. But what if another bike came the other way, or his head hit a boulder, but there weren't any boulders, it was a canal not a river, and how would the boats get past if there were boulders? Facts. But there were no boats coming down this section of the canal, else how would they get past the

Portaloo, and how did it even get in there, and what else lurked beneath?

The blue was gone now, and dark clouds hung low over the locks, the grass banking neat and short like the village green back home where sheep mowed the lawn, but there were no sheep here. She'd have to get Finn off his bike at these bits if she brought him. The black round pools had no bottom. You could go in at this point, sink, nobody would see. She shivered. What were the trees called? The cold air pressed through them and they bowed down like they might fall on the path. She got her jumper out the bag and felt about to see if she'd remembered an umbrella. Up ahead, on a floating jetty, two men sat fishing. One was about 5'5, considerably smaller than her, and he brought to mind the figure and energy of a jockey. He wore brilliant white joggers and a new pair of white trainers that gave him an extra inch or so, no top on, a lean torso not yet golden like his forearms and face. His friend was stouter and all in black, with dark hair gelled into spikes. Even from 20 feet away, she could sense a deep sadness in this guy, just his posture – he looked beat, dead beat. Maybe the small one could feel her ogling because he looked round and waved. She'd started doing that – ogling – now she was past forty, and she found it a humiliating pastime. She might as well start drooling. It was disgusting, and what's more she wasn't accustomed to it, having always thought of herself as prizing the personality and intellect of a person over their looks. This new phase seemed so shallow.

'What do you get out of there?' she said to the men. She wanted to ask them about the weird red animal.

'Tench, carp, pike,' said the small one.

'Trout, if you're lucky,' said the sad one.

'Christ almighty!' said the small one, rolling a plastic bag over his hair as giant spatters of rain started falling. The two men reeled in their lines and ran towards the tall black dookit to the left of the tow path. She ran after them. The sad-looking one fiddled with an elaborate lock system and got the door open.

'Grab that brolly for the lady, it's in the back somewhere,' said the short one. She ran the word 'lady' through her head. It had started happening on buses: 'Give the lady a seat,' or 'Let the lady past.'

'Is this yours? The dookit?' She felt stupid using the word, like she'd stolen something that didn't belong to her.

'My da's. But he's in a home now.'

'Sorry,' she said.

'Don't be.'

Part of the sad one's right ear was missing, like it had been bitten off, and there was a deep five-inch scar at the corner of his mouth. He wore a James Connolly t-shirt.

'I like your top,' she said.

'I got it last time I was over in Ireland.'

'You got family there?'

'Aye. I'm Paul. He's Craig.'

'I'm Chloe,' she said, hating her own name, her own voice. 'I love that sound,' she said, 'of the pigeons.' She rolled her tongue up to the roof of her mouth and puffed out her cheeks, producing a perfect 'roooup roooup.'

The men laughed. 'You want to take a look?' said Paul.

She climbed up the ladders that folded out of the structure

and peered inside. The rain on the tin roof sounded like loud rapturous applause and she'd have liked to have recorded it, but her phone, and it wasn't a place to film, you couldn't have.

'Those are the happy couples,' said Paul, pointing to a series of small clean cages with pairs of pigeons in them. 'Want to see the hen up in the loft? The hens are the girls.'

She nodded and squeezed past the men to climb up. At the top, a white pigeon strutted about, cooing. The rain slowed to a soft patter and the pigeon's coos grew more insistent. It couldn't get out.

Dirt

Sarah Davy

Your mother calls and asks if I've heard anything and I tell her no. There was a sighting, she says, of you on a train in a green mac heading south. You never owned a green mac but I let her cling to its hem.

People come and go, offer words wrapped in barbed wire, crane their necks to peer into the hallway. Premature flowers line the windowsill and the fridge is crammed with Tupperware, leftover meals crumbed in mould.

On bin day, I smile at a neighbour and they call the police. Why would she be smiling, at a time like this? The officer is sympathetic, leaves me another card, will be in touch if they hear anything.

I wait for the sun to come up, to dry dew from the grass so I can kneel, plunge my arms wrist-deep into soil, teasing roots, settling bulbs. This new landscape is mine, a river cut through the concrete prison you built for me. Days unfold in front of me. My forehead is tanned and freckles litter my cheeks.

The neighbour leans over the gate again. I should be inside, draped in black and weeping. Not rain-soaked with soil streaked across my face. I turn the pointed fork over in my hand and smile. Hear her tapping the number on the card and speaking to the police through the open window.

I dream now and sleep through until morning, quilt loose around my shoulders. No pool of sweat or keen pain behind my eyes. There is a space opening up that I never thought existed.

When the first shoots pierce the brown earth, I feel a lightness. The posters are curling in the sun, the response desk wound up. Your mother has stopped calling. There have been no sightings. I did not join the search.

My hands have been preoccupied with dirt.

Angels

Jerry Simcock

I'm getting nowhere with the face, fuck it, that face I have known for so long, that I watched plump up, sag, crease and crinkle, become paper and fade. But yeah, it's important to get it right, your mother as an Angel is important. . .to get that down and not that horribly puffed out, rouged up mask that was the face of some imposter lying there in the coffin.

Relief comes with the hiss of his air brakes. He blasts the klaxon and I chuck the brushes, grab cigs, keys and dosh, rush down the stairs and climb up into the cab. I slam the door, he grins, passes me the spliff, engages gear and pulls off. It's glorious to be so high up above everything, as he manoeuvres along the double-parked street, 'Starman' on the tape. I breathe in his scent, the sweat and the smell of Spanish tobacco, there's a hint of brandy too – no surprise there really. I watch his arms, the way the muscles and sinews stretch and flicker as he moves the wheel. Then we're up the top of Elm Grove and there's the view out over the racecourse to the sea. . .the evening sunlight picking out the seafront and the piers.

– Barley Mow?

– Nah. Oak, I say, thinking we'll avoid bumping into Davey that way. I know where that leads and I'm not up for it. I need to tell him about her, about the visit.

*

In the Oak though, I shift gear and fancy a bit of wild oblivion, like we used to after we first met. I order up Guinness and Bushmills chasers before he can open his mouth. . .he shakes his head, flickers those lashes, we clink the shots, down them and apply our Guinness moustaches.

After the first few it all goes a bit sour. Chris, Pauly and that flounce in and are all over him wanting to hear about the trip and whether he's brought much gear back. So there's no chance to talk and I really want to talk, there's just no chance once he gets settled in with that lot. It's all hectic, loud and suffocating. So I down the chaser, pick his fags off the bar, shove him out the way and huff off, hoping he'll follow. It takes him a bit, but eventually I hear him running. . .and then his hand on my shoulder, hot breath on my neck.

– What the fuck, Jimmy?

– Look, I can't be dealing with that lot, something's happened. I just want you to myself. Sorry. I need to talk to someone and you're the only one.

He shakes his head and does that strange tongue click thing.

– More drama? He gives me a grin. – You're such a queen.

– Oh piss off. . .it's serious.

– Alright then tell, and give us one of my cigs.

We spark up, then, fag in mouth, he puts an arm round me and we saunter off down St James's as I tell him about the Angel, how she dropped down into the room, like she was on wires being manipulated by that old toe-rag Bernard in the flat above. She had wings and they weren't stick-on homemade jobs either, they were kind of mesmerising the way they shimmered and slowly fluttered, sending patterns of sparkling light all around the room. They were electric, alive. . .or maybe alive is the wrong word in the circumstances. She sits on the sofa, asks me if that's a joint I'm smoking, gently lifts it from my fingers, takes a long deep drag, leans back into the sofa and lets the smoke out slowly so it forms small puffs of cloud around us. She smiles.

– I'd really like a gin and tonic, if you've got the doings? she says. – Make it a stiff one, I need it after visiting your Dad. A right state he's in. He's got a cardboard cut-out of some woman off the telly propped up in my chair so she's watching our telly with him. You need to step in Jimmy. He's not right and he wasn't right even before I. . .

She turns to face me full on and smiles, –. . .passed on.

– Jesus Jimmy, what were you on?

– Look ok. . .I'd had a drink and a spliff or two. You know, like I do when I'm painting. She was so real, but also, thinking about it, like a puppet, a kind of real puppet.

He cups my head in his hands.

– You need to take it easy you know. Don't want you going manic, over the top. . .what's the word? You know, like Annie.

– Psychotic? I laugh. – No danger, the teaching keeps me together. On the straight and narrow. You have to keep your head together for that, especially with those kids.

He releases my face from his hands. Maybe that reassured him. As for me, I'm not that certain, things are a bit fragile, not holding together all that well, slowly falling apart, piece by piece.

– Ok, so what's going on? I mean you know she wasn't real, right? So what's up?

– The neighbour rang. That bloke Clive. Don't know how he got my number. He said he tried Susan but couldn't get hold of her, he felt he needed to let us know Dad was behaving a bit strange, acting like he didn't know them when they went round with a pie for him. All the curtains were drawn and he'd locked all the doors, wouldn't let them in the house. He took the pie though.

– Well maybe you are going to have to go down there, you know. . .just for a visit. Size things up.

I shake my head.

– No way, not after all these years. I mean what would we say to each other? He disowned me for Christ's sake.

– Yeah. . .but, you know, death, loss, grief. It kind of blows a hole in all that doesn't it?

There isn't much I can say to that so I leave it and the neon sign flashing Ladies Night pulls us in.

*

Might've known it'd be Don. He stands behind the bar, his usual self, puffing on a fag and waiting for the night to end.

He's been doing this for years. Show night extensions in unlikely locations equals winter holidays in Portugal. The place is a wreck, well past its former glories, but there is something attractive about the cracked Formica bar top. It reminds me of the 'new' kitchen at home when we were kids, and there's a parquet dance floor and a glitter ball. What more do you need?

It's the tired end of drag night. The mood is melancholic but there is love and companionship in the air and Marlene Dietrich singing 'Falling in Love Again'. There are angels present. Middle-aged dragged-up queens, the worse for wear now, and more relaxed about their appearance than they might have been earlier in the evening. Mascara running, wigs askew, sweat washing powder away to make rivulets in creased faces. A couple sit at one of the round tables, one patting the hand of the other as she weeps. There is a sad beauty in it all. We sit at the bar and he orders us a couple of pints.

– Back from Spain? Don says.

– Yeah, long trip. Now it's supposed to be party time and look where I've ended up.

They laugh.

I need a pee and as I step down from the stool Don growls.

– Watch yourself in there, they like young meat these vultures.

They watch me move across the parquet, past two couples who are too enfolded in each other to pay me any attention.

There's no hassle in the gents, just square disinfectant tablets doing a poor job at masking the piss smells.

As I walk out 'Natural Woman' is playing. A lone angel dances in a pale blue satin dress, straps hanging off a tanned old shoulder. This one has lost her wig. She has a crew cut, balding pate and deep blue eyes. She holds her arms open to welcome me in.

– Come on dearie, dance the last dance with me.

She takes my arms and pulls me in, drapes her arms over me and we do a slow dance. . .this feels so good, to be held closely, but gently. As the music stops we step apart. She leans in with her thumbs and gently dabs my eyes.

– Dry your eyes and wash your face. It'll be alright in time, you'll see.

Holes

Joe Waite

Tony's was the only Drill on Cathcart Road. He worked eight till eight Monday to Saturday, and opened Sunday if one of his regulars needed. In the morning, he hopped down the stairs and put on the kettle before unfolding the sandwich board to go out front. The board had an image of a big red drill with the caption: Tony's Drills – Freshen up your head.

*

Mary lived local and she came in for a couple of holes every month.

Just one behind my ear and one in the top please, Tone. I've been aching for this. Ar Mike lost his job and the twins are back with us – Jane is working offshore for the next few months. I can feel it all building up again.

Tony listened as Mary spoke to him in the mirror, before gently pushing the drill through the top of her skull. Green gas came out of the hole and it smelt like old meat in the sun.

Sounds tough, said Tony, cleaning the rod before repositioning it behind her left ear. This side?

Mary looked in the mirror. How did you know?

Swirls of gas drifted to the ceiling and blood dripped to the floor. Blondie's 'Atomic' started on the radio.

Tonight, make it magnificent...

After the last hole Tony wiped his cloth gently over Mary's scalp, then down onto her neck.

All done. How is that for you?

She closed her eyes and sat for a few seconds.

Much better, thanks Tone. She handed him a tenner as she put on her jacket, pulling her hood up as she stepped out into the rain.

There was a queue forming on the bench by the door, some flicking through magazines or watching the tele. Everyone was preoccupied with pain. Tony washed his hands, looking at his face in the mirror. Age lines spidered from his eyes. He took the locket out and shook it gently. The cloud cleared and he could see his family. Jonny was crawling, pushing the block train along the lino floor, the curtainless windows behind him letting in the dusty light. Beneath the window he saw Ginny, sitting with her back to the wall. She had that loose checked shirt on, and he could see the outline of her collarbones. She moved the rosary beads between her fingers. It seemed so long ago, but he could still feel the weight of her head against his shoulder, that hope that she carried.

Can I get a fucking hole over here? I'm blacking out, Tone.

It was Dougie, back again. Next in the queue, and previously hidden by a magazine.

Tony clasped the locket tight, taking a deep breath, feeling the air against his nostrils: keep it together, it is all for them.

Dougie's three holes didn't take long, then Tina, Jacko and Babs all had their turn. Tony moved mechanically but with care. His experience spoke to him and he knew instinctively where to drill. In turn, they left with breezy smiles and their shoulders looked softer.

Next was a new customer, a young boy of about seven who Tony did not notice arrive as he sat silently, leaning against the window. He had to climb up onto the chair and Tony pumped the seat so the boy could see him in the mirror. The boy had a familiarity, but not one you could put your finger on. Perhaps that's why he was missed – his pain just blended in.

*

At eight Tony shut up shop, moving his mop over the vinyl floor, the strands looking like spaghetti in the pools of blood. His mind drifted to the locket and then to his family. The emptiness, creeping up from his toes before rising above his chest, left him feeling dizzy, so he sat in the chair, feeling its support and seeing his reflection. His shoulders sloped and he looked smaller, like a boxer cowering in the corner.

He reached forward to his drill, attaching a 4.5 to its head. He brought it to his temple, focusing on his breath. His left hand clasped the locket and his right hand held the drill, his finger poised on the trigger. He drilled into the side of his skull and let out a sigh, feeling both the day and his worries drift away.

Ashes to Ashes

Anjali Ramayya

Few trees no house survived the path
of the wildfire that exploded
through parched forest and mountain and canyon.
The birds have flown
and a terrible stillness saddens the land.
Where have all the animals gone?
Burrowed, fled or cremated, eye to the sun,
life-breath to the wind.
Shards of charcoaled pines stand witness
against the empty sky
and distant oaks are leached smoke grey.
Still, they will endure.

The big man weeps.
Rakes fingers through rubble and cindered home.
This is where we kept our precious things:
folders, videos, photo albums,
so many memories.
My grandmother's collection of eighteenth-century books,
her handwriting, the unused answering machine

that housed her voice.
They dig a hole, bury a dead kitten.
Ashes to ashes, dust to dust.
We will rebuild, the big man says.
We will endure.

Impressions

Anjali Ramayya

Hot summer's day,
the sky a square of blue.
Debussy on the radio.
Fields of somnolence drowse in pale gold,
stippled with round gleams of hay
astride purple shadows.
And driving past you see
through heavy lids
a flash of chestnut mare
and her foal with flaxen mane.

Batter (Extract)

Natalie Jayne Clark

Next on Isla's list to batter – Donkey. There are many seagulls to be found in the town of Abermay: dozens of them swoop about Main Street and plenty loiter outside Murray's Fish and Chip Shop, but there is just one named Donkey.

They call him that because he is loud, irritating and incessant, and seems to think he's entitled to a bit of land – like the character after whom he is named from *Shrek*. Isla has come to know this creature intimately, could pick his bastardin squawk out from a flock. And often, she does – hears him before she sees him, knows he's on the descent when she hears the pitch change in his voice followed by the smug wee hoot he gives when he lands on the bin on the pavement outside her chippy, just staring in at her with his evil little eyes.

He even lords it over all the other seagulls, looking down on them from the lid of the ash-stained bin. He takes his time, you see. He waits. Donkey's not in amongst the proletariat gulls, scrabbling for the scraps, trying to discern fag end from sausage roll remnants. No, he waits. He waits until there's a hubristic customer who chomps on their meal before they've even left the shop. He waits until they try to open the door with their elbows and hips, balancing the open box of chips on one hand whilst the other hand is busy stuffing their mouth. He waits until the moment they take the step down out of the chippy and onto the pavement, the moment where one foot is still in the air. Then, Donkey flings his wings wide and squawks right at them as loud as his filthy little lungs will let him and before their food's even touched the floor he's grabbed a handful of their meal or even a whole battered haggis or fish.

In a flash of white, he's gone, but not before hovering in front of the chippy window, waving his spoils in front of Isla's face.

Soon, he will meet his crispy end. But she has to catch the big bugger first.

Over the course of several days, she leaves bigger and greasier bits of battered sausage or haggis, or whatever's leftover, outside the front of the shop, and, where possible, keeps the door propped open until Donkey snatches away the hunk of battered goodies. She does it at different times of the day, just in case he is smart enough to work out what she's up to.

One Wednesday evening, after everyone's gone home, and the main street is even deader than it is during the day, she leaves a whole battered sausage on the floor of the café, door hanging wide open. She hides behind the counter, holding an old plastic hand mirror of her mother's just right so she can spy on the patch of floor between the door and bait.

Isla wishes she had brought a puzzle book. She's got a perfectly good one in the flat and is so close to attempting a creep upstairs because she is bored as fuck when. . .there the bugger is.

He hops leisurely along the black and white chequered floor and stops. The peachy red dot at the base of his beak points upwards and around as he surveys the surrounding area. Again, he moves forwards.

He leaps, grabs the sausage in his claws and spins, all in one dastardly devilishly stunning moment, and Isla can't help a frustrated high-pitched scream. He flaps and squawks back from above her head, rocking the sausage from side to side.

In his arrogance, the sausage slips from his grip and whilst he's momentarily distracted Isla sprints like she's never bloody sprinted before to slam shut the café door.

He settles on the countertop as she turns to face him, slowly lowering the blind across the window of the door behind her back.

They wait. Her brain cogs are buzzing alongside each other furiously to come up with what to do next as he cranes back his neck as if to take a huge breath. Then he howls and squawks and screeches and screams, over and over again.

Fuuuuuccccckkkkk. She doesn't want to antagonise the bastard further, or cause concern amongst the neighbours.

Isla grabs the gargantuan garlic mayo bottle and pelts a shot so powerful Donkey is knocked clean over the back of the counter. She maintains the squeezes of sauce, over and over again, the bottle wheezing and her hands cramping under the strain until finally the seagull ceases to struggle.

She realises how firmly the counter edge is digging into her ribs and takes a small step back before walking around the end of the counter. The seagull is all akimbo, comedically, cartoonishly, one wing pinned over its tummy and the other trapped underneath. The feathers are, upsettingly, quite ruined, sodden with white thick sauce.

Just as she tilts her head for a brief moment of sympathy, he starts furiously wiggling, slips and slides up to his clawed feet and tries to flap – but, alas, his wings are fucked and he's pretty much stuck together. Isla leaps and keeps her hands around his neck for exactly as long as it takes for him to die.

The mayonnaise proves a bit of a problem – the cornflour sticks in weird patches and lumps instead of going over smoothly. Isla dabs beaten egg onto the drier bits to help add a bit of consistency. For this, she dips her right hand deep in the bowl of goopy mixed egg and slathers the viscous stuff onto the seagull with glee. It moves in a satisfyingly unpredictable way, dripping and sliming through her fingergaps. She raises each wing in turn and pretends she's washing his underarms, rubbing it in vigorously before delicately, eyes closed, luxuriating in long strokes along the feathered wings.

She turns him over a few times and dunts him up and down in the cornflour again with a satisfying springy bounce. Apart from his craggy jaggy pokey-out bits, it's much like bouncing a ball of elasticated dough.

For a final touch, she rams a soggy gherkin down his beak in a mockery of a suckling pig stuffed with an apple.

She drops Donkey, whole, into the batter bucket and he schloops right in as she pushes him under with her hand. And into the oil he goes!

She uses these first moments in the oil to wash her hands and the sides down, then stands, drinking a cold Irn-Bru from the adjacent fridge, watching as the seagull bobs and crisps.

Isla kens it's unlikely the whole seagull will cook through – these experiments so far have not been about eating – but she intermittently jabs the carcass with the thermometer nonetheless. She's aiming for 75 degrees celsius – just like you would for chicken.

However, the batter soon darkens from Buddha gold to conker nut right through to just damn well burnt, and he's only up to 50 degrees celsius in the middle. Nearly time to fish him out and examine.

Only. . .

This feels wrong already.

She felt a shudder when he squawked his last bastardin squawk.

She feels like someone is watching her.

She turns and sees a silhouette on the blind of the shop's front door and her slatted spoon clatters to the floor.

Prince of Scars

Craig Johnson

You can see it in a boy by the time he's five, Bruce thought as he watched another season of fathers make their way across the sports fields with another season of sons. The men, still tired or hungover from the end of another working week, shielded themselves from the light rain in everything from faded old windbreakers to expensive wool-lined coats, while their boys trotted along beside them like knock-kneed foals in their team jerseys, shorts, and collapsed socks.

One by one each of the fathers greeted the coach – a man who looked just as world-weary as them – and handed over their sons before joining the small congregation of parents behind the sideline a few yards away. The boys were lined up and instructed to run to the other side of the field while passing the ball along the line. They carried out their instructions with the kind of uncoordinated enthusiasm reserved for the young, every one of them blissfully unaware of the passage that lay ahead, a passage all the men looking on had once undertaken in front of their own fathers.

Under the trees, beside the changing sheds, another team

of boys had formed a circle around an overweight man and were following his poor example of high knee lifts. The two teams made their way to the pitch and assembled on either side of the halfway line before taking the field. A short, shrill whistle pierced the air and the examination began.

Bruce took up his usual spot behind the goalposts as the two teams ran up and down the pitch in a loose gaggle. The mothers shouted encouragement while the fathers barked instructions from behind the white line painted atop the lush wet grass. Already he could see the boys who froze as the chaos veered toward them. Sometimes it swept past them, other times it ran straight into them and left them picking themselves up off the ground wide-eyed with shock, unsure whether or not to cry. Many of these boys would keep up the charade for years, making up the numbers, hiding in the pack while trying to impress their fathers or fit in with their friends. But by their teens they would silently drop away one by one as the bodies of the boy warriors grew thick and raw boned and the tackles were delivered with ever-increasing weight and menace. Some who were callow at first would improve a great deal, but not enough to go anywhere in the game. There were too many others born with courage in spades. Boys who'd hone their skills and harden themselves across countless Saturdays, who'd grow blind to the chaos and deaf to the slap of skin and dull clunk of bones colliding at high speed. Theirs were the only names and numbers that men like Bruce would jot down in their notebooks.

By the time the game was over, each son would give his father the answer he required without a word being uttered.

For the boy who threw himself into the fray his father's nod or affectionate scruff of the hair was the reward. For the boy who hesitated, or worse, shied away, it all depended on the man. Some drew their son in with an arm around the shoulder and a few kind words of encouragement. Others turned and headed back towards the car park, putting a small distance between themselves and their sons.

Near the end of the club season, Bruce would contact the parents concerned and inform them of their son's selection in the representative team. Gushing mothers and proud-as-punch fathers would thank him sincerely before they rushed to bring their son to the phone. It often seemed that the boy himself was the least bothered member of his entire family. But despite the air of teenage indifference Bruce could still feel the young man's delight radiating down the line.

The team would assemble and spend a couple of weeks training for tournaments in which they would clash with boys from other regions of the country who were just as quick and courageous. But even during these tournament days, when the rugby grounds fairly brimmed with reckless doppelgangers, a few boys would separate themselves from the pack with a physicality and guile that made them seem beyond their teenage years.

Sometimes, just once in a while, two of these rare breeds travelling in opposing directions would meet. They would start the game charging like roaring stags, hell-bent on making the other step away first. But it seemed as if each was only lifted by the other's aggression. As the game wore on spectators became enthralled as they bore witness to the struggle unfolding. Even other team members became bit players in the two-man war.

There was a moment, usually deep into the eighty minutes of the match that Bruce waited for, when the two boys had run and tackled themselves to a standstill. The instant when the test slid from physical to mental and the question became who would be willing to endure the battle the longest. This was the point where one boy would show the other that it was useless, that he might as well give in, because he would always drag himself up off the ground and charge again. He would never let himself be bested, regardless of the scoreboard.

That was the boy Bruce looked for.

Last Orders

Sophie Leslie

We held hands until it was time to leave. I tucked the thin blanket and sheet around his body and laid his hands across his chest. The shutters were open and the sun shone in the small, healthy garden. Looking out the window I saw a couple taking a short stroll. That used to be us, I thought, the Before Us.

"It's time," said the nurse on the phone this morning.

The journey was familiar and I arrived quickly, sinking into the familiar spongy plastic chair next to his bed. An adhesive medical patch sent painkillers into his arm and on his nightstand there were photos of us as a young family.

We had bounced about for a while: here, home, here, home again; until we ended up back here. But here was now a different here, a last-stop here, where death was normalised and pain handled with care.

I held his hand until I knew.

I took a few steps out of the room and called a nurse. Everyone said the hospice had a wonderful staff and a pleasant setting where remaining life was enjoyed.

Because death is normal, completely normal.

As I walked home I passed the Before Us, having another stroll in the cultivated garden.

I fingered the blister packet in my pocket and felt the pills ripple against my skin. "Diazepam," said the GP. "It will help stabilise your emotions. It's a popular choice these days, nothing to be ashamed of."

Later that night, as I lay in bed staring at the ceiling, I pulled a blanket and sheet closely round my body, and laid my hands across my chest.

Wrang Words

Nicole Le Marie

Words worm and bury
                      passing soil tae grit
the mistake is caching grubs
                      rattling in yer heid
gnawing in yer tum.

Chuck them an the pyre
                      keek them spiral up
ashen whispers tae the sky
                      that ye've haud
enough.

Catch a cindered thought
                      moth's wing dust by touch
be gan
        be doun
                grain awe life;

normal ye'll become.

The Parable of the Pangolin

Dom Howell

Her name was Cgoise and she believed that, in times gone by, the animals talked like us. She was quite serious about it. Even if you had your doubts there was something about the way she spoke that carried you along.

Her house was different to the other houses in the village because she'd painted the walls purple and dug a border all around it and planted flowers.

Sometimes she'd sit outside on a chair in the sun and feed the goat from her hand. I remember there was a spade with a plastic green handle propped up near the front door and on the back of the handle it said MADE IN CHINA and to this day I've always wanted to go there.

In the evening I would sit on the floor next to the fire in the main room and she would chat to me with a pangolin balled up on her knees. She would tell me to watch the pangolin. It had tiny black eyes and a long pink tongue like a shoelace.

"One day you will need the skin of a pangolin," she'd say.

I didn't know exactly what she meant but I felt it to be true.

*

She was friends with a man called Mr Xgaiga. He had a beard and square glasses that he'd made himself. Cgoise called Mr Xgaiga an artist and he wore bright clothes and liked to dance. He'd shuffle up behind her when she was cutting limes, put a hand on her waist and they'd start swaying to the radio. They danced free and barefoot and with their arms in the air. It made me want to jump about and tap the silver salad bowl with a fork.

Whenever Mr Xgaiga came round Cgoise would put on different clothing, or change her earrings, or sometimes she might redden her lips a touch but it was nothing too obvious. She kept it casual, and I liked that.

Occasionally he'd play cricket with me out the back while she'd watch and sip beer on her chair. The ground was hard and perfect for off-cutters and leg breaks.

He had a slinky action and would bowl to me over and over again until I could cut the blade of the bat through the meat of the ball. It's funny, even though he trained me up, I was never picked for the school team.

"Good times don't last forever," I remember Cgoise saying to me one night. We were staring into the fire together when she said it, and the pangolin was at her feet. I saw deep cracks in her heels.

Not long after that Mr Xgaiga stopped playing cricket with me. He never had the energy. Things were changing in the village, he said. He spent a lot of time at the Cooka Boo health centre, and me and Cgoise would be left to sit and draw. Her lines were always cleaner and bolder and simpler than mine.

"Whatever marks you make, I am proud of those marks," she'd say.

But with Mr Xgaiga absent, she kept having to leave. And I'd have to sit there finding it hard to draw without her.

It got lonely. Really lonely. And I started to do bad things.

I used loads of firewood. Drank her bottles of beer. Then I hit her homemade limoncello.

I vomited one night round the back of the house. I was lying down staring up at the stars when I heard a shuffling. It was the pangolin. The moonlight reflected off its armour and it came and nestled neatly into my arm, resting its head on my chest.

"Look," I whispered, "A shooting star."

The pangolin lifted a tiny eyebrow. "Doubt it," it said.

"D'you mean?"

"Far too consistent for a shooting star. Much more likely to be a satellite."

I didn't speak. There was no wind.

"You know," said the pangolin, "the more you come here, the less you'll be where you are."

I didn't know what he meant, but I felt it to be true.

*

The next day Cgoise came back to the house. She had a haste about her. She found me lying under the kitchen table asleep, the pangolin curled in her armchair. She said Mr Xgaiga was getting worse. Lines moved in her brow. Then she asked me about the firewood. The limoncello. The vomit. She said I needed to do better, but then said, "My child" and placed a hand on my forehead. It felt warm and strong and good. I closed my eyes and saw shooting colours in the dark. I remembered the pangolin's voice. The more you come here, the less you'll be where you are.

"Mr Xgaiga needs us to dig deep for him," Cgoise said, snapping me back into the room. I heard the jangle of her bracelet as she picked up the pangolin and lolled it over her shoulder, its tail coiling around her neck.

"Draw me hope," she said, "there's fresh mopane worms in the fridge."

She closed the door and I was left alone again. I drew all night and snacked on the crunchy worms in a spicy dipping sauce. I drew satellites in the night sky. I drew waves. Sea storms over cities, but if you looked closely you could see tiny skilful surfers having the time of their lives.

I fell asleep with my head in my elbow and when I lifted it next morning, I saw Cgoise opening the door gently, white light behind her. Then Mr Xgaiga walked in. He looked thin, but he was smiling. I ran to him and we hugged. Cgoise came over and put her arms round both of us.

"We are home," she said. "No more trips to the Cooka Boo please God."

It made me happy to see them like this, but I had a question. I sensed Cgoise didn't want me to ask it.

After a few hours I couldn't help it.

"Where is he?" I asked. "The pangolin?"

Mr Xgaiga patted the cushion next to him and I went over and sat down, feeling the warmth of his side.

"Always respect the pangolin," he said. "He is in a better place now." He moved a finger upwards. "I owe him my life."

When they'd gone to bed, I could hear snores and Mr Xgaiga occasionally coughing. I crept into the kitchen and saw Cgoise's lilac handbag looped over a chair.

I peeked inside and found a leaf of pangolin armour. Just one grey panel of it. I picked it up, felt its thickness, its smoothness, and then had the urge to hold it to my forehead. A shudder came over me.

I went to the front door, opened it and started running.

Case Study

Martin Geraghty

Thirs a puddle ae urine wi a white shoelace in the middle ae it. A wonder wit came first – wis thir a random shoelace somedae decided ti pish oan fir a laugh or did somedae look at the puddle ae urine an couldnae resist drappin a shoelace in it?

Ma auld man is jigglin thi shrapnel in his pocket as he checks wit floor we're at. 10. . .12. . .14. The lift doors open an we're mugged wi the reek ae a mingin cocktail ae disinfectant fightin fir superiority wi soup waftin fae a neighbour's. A cover ma gub an shuffle behind da.

He opens the door an heads straight ti his bedroom ti look fir wit he calls his "credentials" – the policy documents thit'll pay fir everythin, the spread after it, the whole shebang.

A let him hiv his privacy an head ti the livin room. Av no been back here fir years. Ah move ti the windae an watch wee figures scuttlin aroon gon aboot their daily business. Wit the fuck ir these people playin at? Ah hear the rumblins ae an aeroplane an watch it fly o'er us until it disappears roon aboot the John Brown shipyards. Couldnae tell yi wit kind ae plane it wiz cos ma mind wiz fixed oan the ignorant bastards gon oan holiday at a time like this. A kick the skirtin board a few rapid ti stop me fae punchin the windae. Press ma palms an face against the windae an close ma eyes. It's still vibratin fae the rumble ae the aeroplane. Am disturbed wi da shoutin fae his bedroom thit he's ready an tellin me ti wait in the landin.

The people actin like everythins normal an the holidaymakers are still loiterin in ma mind so a don't notice he's there until he places the suitcase oan the floor next ti me. Ma auld man's life in a tacky red suitcase a hivnae seen fir o'er 30 years. An it fuckin launches me back ti the first time he lifted me inside it an shoved it doon a flight ae stairs. An a mind wonderin why wi had a big red suitcase when naebdae had ever been oan a holiday afore. Ah hink back ti aw the fun wi had wi the suitcase that summer – zoomin doon the stairs fir hours every day til the week afore gon back ti school when ma auld dear got in fae work an put the kibosh oan it by sendin da packin. An ah watched him, head bowed as he carried the suitcase doon the garden path. When he turned roon ah planked ma face intae ma auld dear's cheesecloth dress an begged her ti let him come back. The tears wirnae cos he wiz leavin, but he wiz leavin wi ma new favourite toy – an ah wondered if ad ever see it again.

Ma auld man is standin at the lift tellin me ti get a move oan.

A cannae say a word or make eye-contact. An a cannae chase away aw the mad heavy-duty memory stuff. Aw a kin hink aboot is kickin that fuckin suitcase up an doon the landin.

Disappearing

Sneha Subramanian Kanta

This particular part of the city is like a pomegranate aril. It goes unnoticed like the moon above a traffic jam-speckled highway. Every evening, the city gets new lights, sprawling like the artificial illumination on advertisement boards.

There were not many trees on main roads, except in routes full with residential buildings. Every tree bough has thick coatings of dust from vehicular traffic. Many years later, she will realize that these were the years of dust.

In the afternoon, she looks at the flutter of taxicabs in the lane outside a coffee shop. Many years later, the coffee shop won't be there. The road will look desolate with one building where office-goers arrive, and street vendors begin setting up stalls.

Her friend from another country calls up and says, "You've been reading too much of *Mrs Dalloway*." Every time the friend mentions this, she thinks about rivers, stones, the body of Woolf floating in the Ouse, and the material quality of things.

Dead End

Catriona Shine

My mother has been ready to go since yesterday. The woman who should come and fix her up was sick, they said, and they had nobody else. It was the same everywhere I rang. It was the wrong time to die. They told me how to tie her mouth closed, and they said they could make the trip out one time only and they would have to take her straight to the graveyard. We're waiting for them now.

Yesterday, before anyone came, I put her in her travelling clothes. She hardly went anywhere, and made a big deal of any trip. I packed her a little case with her favourite things and put it beside her on the bed. The translucent china cup she used for her homemade herbal tea is in there. She rarely washed it, so neither did I. She can bring the flavour with her. I should have packed the teapot too, but there's no space left, and they're all here now. I put in her waterproof boots and a compass. There was room for her gardening gloves and the smallest of her trowels. I put in a map, but it only stretches to the edge of the county. I couldn't find a map of the stars. There's one here, somewhere. I realise that many of the things I've packed are what I'll need to survive here, but it seemed wrong to part her from them. I tried to get her hand to close around the strap of the case, but her fingers had stiffened, and I was afraid I would break them. I've never touched a dead person before.

When my aunt Maureen came, she changed the sheets and put a blanket over my mother as if she was only sleeping. It didn't work. My mother was a living creature in sleep, snoring and retorting, resettling.

My mother's sisters each had a two-hour drive, from different directions, but they got here yesterday evening while I was still ringing around funeral homes. Maureen was the first to arrive. She came alone, but her family are on their way. My uncle Mick had to pick up my three cousins first. They're all older than me, in college and just finished for the summer. My aunt Gertie and uncle Gerry and their daughter, little Grace, came soon after. Grace is fourteen, I think. She's their only child. Adopted. The four of them stayed with me all night, and no one slept, but we took turns lying on the couch and on my bed.

Gertie has gone off again. She said she was going to the florist. She said she would go alone, needed to be alone.

Maureen has been dusting and tidying since she came, moving things out of their usual places, rearranging cushions and trinkets. She's doing it one-handed now, checking her phone every few seconds.

They'd want to hurry on, she says, and Gertie too. The hearse will be here before them.

There's no reception, says Grace.

Don't worry, says Gerry, we still exist when we're offline.

He's funny, Gerry. Gertie's nice too. I'd choose them over

Maureen and Mick if I was choosing new parents for myself. It would even things out, since Maureen already has three children. That's the reason I'd give. I've played out this scenario a million times since my father disappeared. It's best to have everything worked out in advance because, when you're alone, you might not think straight. As it is, I'm starting college in a couple of months so, in a funny way, everything can continue according to plan – not that anything can be funny right now, or maybe it's the opposite, maybe everything is completely ridiculous.

The house has been on the market for months. Nobody wants it, or even knows where it is. That's what Gerry said when he arrived. We almost drove past, he said, didn't see it, looked right through it. He was being doubly funny. You can't drive past a dead end – and it's a glass house. It has a normal flat roof, but every single wall in the place, inside and out, is composed of huge sheets of glass. My mother used to explain to people that the glass lets the bog in, so we can live as part of it, and we don't have a problem with nosy neighbours. Some shelves and cabinets are politely placed around the bathroom. A slender army of steel columns keeps up the roof and prevents this crystal from crashing down around us. The metal creaks in warm weather, but the sun hasn't come out since I got home from boarding school two weeks ago.

It was odd creeping here in a taxi, instead of bouncing over the bog road in the Fiat with my mother. I was never sure if she enjoyed the speed, or just wanted the trip to be over. It was also strange to come directly home. When the taxi bypassed the nearest small town, I knew, at last, this was an emergency. My mother always stopped off somewhere for a treat: lunch in a hotel lobby where she would raise a morsel on her fork and ask the waitress, What's this here? And this? Or a dash around an art gallery. She would point at framed photos and bog-oak sculptures, explaining them like a local, but I knew she rarely visited. She would gulp down all a country town could offer in one hour and then bring me home.

We're off the grid, as my mother put it, solar-powered, a lantern in the wilderness. It's a hilly, tufty, bushy kind of place, with the same texture as far as I've ever wandered. If you were drawing it from above, you could take an area of, say, fifty square metres, which contains all the essential elements – swathes of hissing heather, patches of exposed turf, moss, a bog-hole of brown acidic water, a lump of bog oak, a forgotten tool, a lone and half-dead blackthorn – and rotate and repeat this representative sample as far as the edge of the drawing. There's nothing but a stream to guide you, if you were trying to find this place going cross-country, but this is not something that anybody attempts.

Maureen is currently bawling by my mother's bed. I need the loo, but I'm afraid to leave in case she throws herself over my mother and covers her in unwanted tears. Mom didn't like when people were showy with their feelings. Maureen eventually splutters something about sandwiches and goes out.

Gerry sees the gap and comes to hover beside me, tickling the bedspread.

If there's anything we can help with, Aoife, now or later,

he says, I just want you to know that you can always ask. We're here for you.

Will you teach me to drive? I say.

We both look out at my mother's maroon-coloured Fiat, tucked away in a corner of the front yard, under a clawing hawthorn. It's mine now, but I don't have a licence. This is a bit of a mismatch, because I know all about cars, and my main intersection with the world has been the drives from here to boarding school and back, a few times a term.

Gerry looks over his shoulder, like there might be a better driving instructor standing right behind him. He's been casting furtive glances in strange directions ever since he got here, and I thought it was the reflections that were getting to him. It's as if he sees something that's not there, as if this is some sort of haunted house. The last time he was here was when my father went missing. Gerry was the only one who went looking for him. He went to all the shops on the pile of receipts he found in the glove compartment of the Fiat. He didn't find my father, but at least he tried. Everyone else called his disappearance desertion. I was so young, I thought they were talking about the spreading of the Sahara, and he had gone to fix it. I once overheard someone say, He ran off on them. My mother said that wasn't true.

It's reassuring to know where my mother is. At least I can be certain she's dead. That's second place to knowing she's alive.

Not knowing is the worst, I say.

I don't know about teaching you, says Gerry. He has his hands raised, like he can't decide whether to hug me or pat me on the shoulder. Maybe you should have a drink, he says.

Gerry!

Maureen is standing in the doorway with a platter of sandwiches, and she knows not to bring food in here.

A small whiskey or something, he says.

All she needs is a cup of tea.

Grace is folded up in an armchair, reading a book of poetry she found on the shelf, and lifting her brow now and then towards the road.

I should have gone with Mom, she says. Why is she taking so long?

Don't worry, says Gerry, going over to sit on the arm of her chair, and messing with her hair.

He removes a whiskey glass from the coffee table as Maureen puts down the platter, as if the two are incompatible.

They should be here by now, all of them, says Maureen. She shakes her phone and looks at the screen to see if it's helped. What's the hold up? she says.

She looks at the whiskey glass in Gerry's hand, and he takes a sip. We all look out along the road, and then we each take a triangle of sandwich and look at our laps. I hadn't thought I was organising a wake, but that's what this has turned into, ceremonial waiting. I nibble a corner of my sandwich which is overloaded with lumps of butter, too cold to spread.

Look, says Grace.

We all rise at once, but there's no car coming, only a dense fog, creeping in the same way we had all arrived. It gets foggy around here a lot. Sometimes you get drenched just walking through it. My mother used to go out purposely to soak in it. A fog bath, she called it. Anything could turn magical in her mind.

The strange thing about this particular fog is that it's moving so fast. I can see it folding around the two cars, fog fingers claiming them for itself. The others point at it and say holy words and curses. Grace and Gerry are glued to each other. Maureen has the wherewithal to slide the front door closed, but there are windows open. The fog wraps itself around the whole house. We're in a pillow but there's no comfort in it, only sudden shivers and cold sweat on my spine, and a strange metallic smell – something rusty. Grace screams and stands up on the armchair as the fog trails in along the floor. Maureen blesses herself repeatedly and reels off an incorrect version of the Hail Mary. I'm halfway over to my mother's room before I notice I'm walking, only alerted by the wet chill at my ankles. When I reach her side, I hold onto the bed with the strange idea that I must stop her getting swept away.

After a short spell, it's gone, and we can see outside again. We turn and watch the fog continue on its way, a roving cloud licking the bog.

Dribbles of condensation run down the glass, inside and out, and I get a cloth to dry it off. I want to use soap and vinegar, to swab it all away, because there is nothing cleansing about this residue. This is evaporated quagmire, foul and contaminated.

Maureen tries to help, but she uses the floor cloth and smears dirty loops around the glass. Gerry and Grace both have their feet tucked under them on the couch and they are whispering to each other.

I slide open the front door again and look out to see if there's any sign of the hearse, which they promised would be here hours ago. Something is wrong. I can see the thick frames of my glasses, as well as their foggy edges, but I put up a hand and feel for them all the same, because the road is – the road – I mean, it can't–

I go outside, cross the concrete slab of the yard. I stop at the edge and look out to where the road should be, but there's nothing. No road, no hole or gap where the road used to be, nothing.

A few days ago, when Mom had weakened but was still alive, I jogged up the road a stretch and back again. My soles still recall the gravelly give of it, but where the road used to be is tufty and bushy now. It's as if it was never here.

Gerry's standing to my right, and the others beyond him are stretched out along the edge of the concrete, scared to step onto the turf.

I thought the road was on this side, says Gerry.

It is, says Maureen. You're drunk.

You're both drunk, says Grace. The flipping road's on the other side of the house.

We all walk around the house, Maureen and I going clockwise, Grace and Gerry going anti-clockwise, always in sight on account of the glass walls. We pass each other wordlessly at the rear of the house and circle back to the front yard.

Maureen stretches her arm up and waves her mobile in the air. I ask her what network she's on and tell her she can use my phone, but it only works from one spot in the sitting room.

Grace and Gerry are back at the edge of the slab, standing at the right spot now, but pointing in slightly different directions.

It started here all right, says Gerry, but then it curved away in that direction, remember?

No, says Maureen, it swerved away to the right at that hollow there.

Does anyone have a compass? says Grace.

I'll check, I say.

Back inside, I go straight to Mom, and I speak in a low voice and ask her what the heck is going on. She lies there as if everything is fine.

Maureen tries the funeral home on my phone, but nobody answers. She pockets my phone, absentmindedly.

Her Toyota Corolla starts up, with Gerry behind the wheel, and Grace beside him. Maureen rushes outside, screaming, Get out of there, you fools!

They drive past her, off the edge of the concrete. The car humps along a short way, flattening a few scratchy bushes, and then the nose sinks and the rear end of the car goes up in the air. The passenger door opens, and they both tumble out that side and help each other up. They don't look like they want to come back to us, but Maureen says, Just leave the car. Leave it, and get back here, quick.

I almost expect them to run away, but they come back, choosing each step with care.

*

Maureen has redialled the funeral home and every member of her family several times, to no avail, and now Gerry takes my phone from her and it's the police he rings. He tells them to rescue us. He says the road sank into the bog. He says, We can't wait. We have a body to be buried. We were waiting for the hearse to come when the road disappeared.

Maureen and Grace lean in close to him, to hear what's being said.

It sank, yes, he says. I don't know why. This is a bog.

There's a long pause, and then Gerry says, No, we haven't, no, I suppose we could try. Right, I'll call back and let you know.

He hangs up.

She said to walk out to where the road starts, and they'll send someone to pick us up from there, or she said we could just call a taxi.

Maureen gasps. She swipes her phone, then taps a number into mine and orders a taxi.

They'll be forty minutes, she says, and makes for the kitchen.

We'd better see about this road then, says Gerry. I'll go.

Grace follows him out, and, when he squelches away, she sits at the edge of the slab like it's a bench. I lean my forehead against the glass, to watch. He makes slow progress, hopping from tuft to tuft. He has the right angle at first, but then he veers just a little too much to the left.

Sure won't we see the taxi coming? says Maureen, behind me, tapping a spoon off the edge of her cup, and depositing her weight into the puffy armchair.

I look at the point on the crest of the hill where the road used to pass by a tree. There's no road all the way out there.

Maureen's on her second cup of tea when Gerry disappears over the horizon. Grace sees it too and gets up from her viewing point. Maureen calls her in for a cup of tea, but she shakes her head and starts to loop the house. If she was going clockwise, I might have been okay with it, but it's irritating the way she circles us again and again, and I worry that she might be unscrewing us. I pull a chair up close to Mom's side and tell her everything will be all right.

Maureen makes noises in the toilet that walls like these could not possibly be expected to absorb. When she comes out, she says, You might give me a hand tidying up, Aoife.

There's a pile of cups and saucers staining the wood on the coffee table, and she's the only one who's been drinking tea, but I do as she asks. She's a heavy version of Mom, coarser too. Crockery and glasses always seem to clatter in her sturdy hands.

Grace has a bluish tinge at the edges of her face when she comes back inside, and her arms are all goosebumps.

I want to ring Mommy, she says.

No love, says Maureen, she forgot her phone, remember? She left it here.

Well, why doesn't she call us? Why doesn't she call your phone, Aoife? Why isn't she worried about me?

She wouldn't know my number off by heart, I say.

Maureen puts a blanket over Grace's shoulders. One of Mom's fair hairs is on it, straight as an exclamation mark.

I ring the funeral home again, and this time a woman answers. She says they tried to come out but couldn't find us. She says she can't understand it, Jimmy knows all the by-roads. I tell her about the road sinking into the bog and she says, Sweet mother of God, how were we supposed to find you without a road?

I ask her how far they got, and she calls out, Jimmy! Jimmy! without covering the mouthpiece and then she tells me they couldn't find the turn-off.

They couldn't find the turn-off, I tell the room.

That's a mile away, says Maureen.

It's three kilometres, says Grace.

The woman on the phone says, Is there someone there with you? Can you send someone out to the main road? Go to the nearest house and ring us, and we'll see what we can do. 'Twill be tomorrow now anyway before we can do the burial. Half the day's gone.

Dad! shouts Grace, running outside but halting at the edge of the slab.

We could walk out to meet him, but we stay here, close to the house. Grace waves frantically to him, and calls out, Dad! Dad! as if there was a chance he wouldn't see the only house between here and the horizon. He's been gone for over an hour, plenty of time to reach the main road, though he is moving slowly, and I wonder if he chickened out and turned too early.

He collapses onto the concrete, as if it's some kind of holy ground. Grace kneels beside him.

I couldn't find it, he says. I walked for ages, but I couldn't find it.

Were you going in the right direction? says Maureen. Aoife, tell him which way he should have gone. You go with him, Aoife, she says.

Go by yourself, Aoife, says Grace. Leave Dad here with me.

I'm not leaving Mom.

Take Auntie Maureen with you.

I'm not leaving her, I say.

All right, says Maureen, calm down. Gerry, come on with me. The children can stay here.

I point out the tree at the crest of the hill and tell them to make for that and keep going straight on from there. You'll cross a stream, I say, you'll cross the same stream twice. It swings around. Straight on over the following hill and you should see the main road.

Gerry's shoes are drenched, but I have nothing to offer him. Even my socks would be tiny on him. Maureen puts plastic bags inside her shoes, and they set off.

I go back to Mom's side, where nothing has changed.

Grace comes and stands at the foot of the bed. There's a smell of vanilla off her, but her shoulders are heaving like one of those possessed children in horror films.

It's your mother's fault, she says.

She marches off outside, bringing a blanket to her lookout spot this time. I can see her from anywhere I sit or stand. Maybe due to Maureen's influence, I feel a need for warmth between my palms. I brew a pot of Mom's herbal tea. I do it just as Mom did, but it smells different, more acidic. Maureen already has the insides of the pot tarred with the black tea she brought with her. I bring two mugs of it outside and place them between us on the edge of the slab.

I wait until she slurps her tea.

Grace, I say, I don't know if you remember, when we were young, that summer at Auntie Maureen's. . .

I remember, she says, putting the mug back down.

We didn't mean it, I say. We were young too.

She has her eyes on her father. She has this privilege.

We were only messing, I say. I can't believe you took us seriously.

You told me they were going to send me back, she says.

It was meant as a joke. It was Peggy's idea. They were older than me. I just went along with them.

I ran away.

I know. We searched for you, Grace. We left notes for you in all the hide-outs, biscuits too. That was my idea.

Yes, well, thanks for the cookies. Can we stop talking about this?

You ate them.

They didn't bring a torch, she says, and I follow her gaze.

We shift our legs under us at intervals. I bring out cushions, and Grace never says thanks, only accepts what I give her as something she deserves.

It's almost dark when they reach the horizon, but I can make out their hunched silhouettes beside the tree.

They're on track, I say. They're going the right way, so far.

The song of a single bird cuts away as the tree fades from sight. We look into the darkness for hours, and then we move inside. We keep all the lights on, to make sure they will see us on their return, but reflections fill the walls, making anything outside impossible to see. I fall asleep on the chair beside Mom, my head on the blanket at her side. When I wake, I see that Grace has dozed off too, on the couch, a rug stuffed between her knees.

As the sun comes up, I see them returning, thin shadows distorting the heather.

They wave to show they have seen us, and we boil water and wait on the concrete with our arms full of blankets for them.

They look terrible. Perhaps I've been staring at Mom's pale face too long, because Maureen and Gerry look pink to me. They're shivering, and their clothes are wet through. They say they walked for ages, straight ahead, over the hill by the tree, a straight line all the way. They walked continually all night, didn't stop to sleep, and just before it got bright, they saw the house again.

It doesn't make sense, says Maureen.

We never turned back, says Gerry.

Round and round in circles, says Grace, and they stare at her. Gerry stands up against her like he wants to hug her but his arms won't lift. I put a blanket over their shoulders, and they turn together and move towards the house.

I run a shallow bath of warm water as Maureen pulls off her wet tights. I wonder who's looking after who.

Do you want a sprig of lavender in it? I say. Mom always put in some herbs, or moss.

She had some strange ideas, says Maureen.

Gerry rings the police again. He screams and curses and tells them they have to save us. He tells them we'll die out here.

We have our kitchen garden, I say, and a good store of tinned food.

Grace and Gerry huddle together with the phone at Gerry's mouth. Send a helicopter, he says. It's no prank. I have a child here, he says. I need to get her to safety.

I watch Maureen put on Mom's unwashed dressing gown. She comes and takes my phone from Gerry, and gives the directions to the turn-off. She puts the phone face-down on the table and says, They're sending out a squad car.

They won't find us, says Grace.

Her voice is hoarse and muffled. She's talking into her father's shoulder. He tells her she's safe here, that he won't leave her alone again, that the police will come and get us, as soon as they realise it's serious. They're just slow, he says.

She disentangles herself and goes out the back door, and outside is no hiding place so I know she's crying, but I don't look that way.

She's right, says Gerry. Even if they find the turn-off, they won't be able to drive out here. That's why I told them to send a helicopter.

You didn't convince them, though, did you? says Maureen.

I did all I could.

Good God, she says, I don't know, but they'll have to get us out of here some way or other.

We hear a bang from the outhouse and Grace emerges, carrying a shovel and a spade, one in each hand like two staffs. In her green tunic, she looks like a modern-day St Patrick. She props them up against the back door and comes inside.

No, I say, and I stand, barring the door to Mom.

We have to leave, she says. If we go together, nobody will get lost.

Listen to her, Aoife, says Gerry. There's something going on here.

I've noticed.

It's her, says Grace, pointing to Mom. There's a spell on the place. I know it.

We'll bring Mom with us, I say.

Everyone says, No, but I won't be swayed, and they need my sense of direction.

We use the dining table as a stretcher. We screw off the legs and then change our minds and screw them back on, because it's a long walk and we'll have to put it down when we can. We pack Mom in with old coats and sleeping bags, and tie her cocoon to the table with a length of coarse rope. We each take hold of a corner.

I close the windows and doors, but leave all the lights on.

When we get to the tree at the crest of the hill, we put down the table and pass around a plastic bottle of water. We rotate, so Maureen and Gerry are the front pallbearers going down the hill.

I point the way and we go on.

We cross the stream and walk into a fog at the other side.

We cross the stream again. I'm wearing my wellies; the others were drenched long ago.

Straight on this way, I say.

The fog fades but doesn't disappear. Grace and I switch position to distribute the pain evenly on our bodies.

We cross the stream again and Mom slides on the table because I halt so suddenly.

No, I say, no. We're not meant to cross another stream.

Do you even know where we are? says Grace.

I point back where we've just come from. It's that way, I say. We've looped around somehow.

Nobody complains. We turn around.

Pick a point on the hill and walk towards that, says Maureen, that's what we'll do.

Grace groans under the weight, and Gerry tells her it won't be long now.

It gets dark, and the dim line of the hill before us fades away. We keep walking. All our phones die, as does the torch, and the moon slips behind the clouds. We come to a stream again, and cross it this time, cross another one, keep walking, not thinking, just walking, ready to walk on, no matter how long it takes. We'll cross the country if we must.

There's a light ahead.

A house, says Grace, and she abandons her corner to run towards it. The others let go too and stumble after her, but I hold my corner steady.

I know those lights.

Tight Lines

Mandy Watson

I was on my own, like. Wee Eck had called off last minute. Some family thing. As per. Anyhows, we had the usual beat on the Tay booked and I couldny find anyone else to take Eck's place at short notice. So, I was on my lonesome and it was miserable. Pishing down like. I hadny had a single bite all day. I was just thinking of giving it up for a game of soldiers when I remembered that fancy new spinner and thought I'd give it a wee go. I cast it long and let it play out for a bit. A few seconds later. Fuck me. I felt a tug. Ya beauty.

Aye right! Soon as I started reeling in, I knew. No movement. No fight back. Just heavy. This was no trout. Probably a bit of rubbish. People chuck all sorts in the rivers. Shoes, coats, bin bags of kittens. Ignorant bastards. I'd no choice but to reel it in now but I decided to take it easy, make sure the line didny break. Then at least I'd have cleared a bit of crap out the water.

I managed to get the net under it but I still couldny work out what it was. Something furry? On the bank, I tipped the net out on to the grass. I gave it a poke and it squelched.

It looked like dark brown fur. I felt a wee bit sick, like. Thinking mibbe it was a dead animal. Somebody's wee dug? I turned it over and nearly fell out my waders laughing. A monkey.

Aye, a toy monkey. Its wee chimpanzee face smiling up at me. Sodden brown fur with pink face, ears, hands, feet. Fair made my day. I wished Eck had been there. I thought about taking it home for him. To cheer him up, like. But the thing was wringing and stinking, so I chucked it in the flatbed and later dumped it next to a bin on the A9 when I stopped for a piss.

I was nearly home when Eck phoned to ask, "Any luck the day, mate?"

"Aye. . .as a matter of fact. . ."

Reckoning

Regi Claire

I put my hand down a toilet
down the throat of a dog
down the pants of a man
& I mewled kitten-thin

& I laughed & I sang
the wrong song the wrong laugh
& I cried like a girl like a boy
& I mewled kitten-thin

& I cooked & I burnt
& I heated & I sweated
& I bled & I shat
& I mewled kitten-thin

& I screwed & I blew & I licked
& I came & I went
said *again* & *again*
& I mewled kitten-thin

then one night I ran
& I jumped & I roared
& I swore & I tore

so now this is me
I am here I am safe
like a skull in a cradle

a newborn in a cave

LINDA MCCARTNEY

David Bowie From Linda's Pictures 1977
Screenprint on paper
34 x 33.3 cm
Tate. Presented by Rose and
Chris Prater 1978
© Linda McCartney

MARK II

Caoimhín de Paor

For Paul

We must make a queer sight, myself and my father, stood up upon the hedgerow and still as statues of a Sunday morning. We're missing Mass, but that's alright. Dad has cleared it with the almighty upstairs – Mam herself.

We're here for a different kind of worship. Dad in a motorsport jacket, a hodgepodge of block colours, and me in a windbreaker too big for me, my hands not quite making it out the sleeves. I'm glad of it though. It's raining buckets and the trees are soaked, their great leaves drooping for the earth. My shoulders are numb from bracing against it. *It'll be worth it,* Dad repeats.

When you're still for this long, nature fills back in around you. The briars rebound in stop-motion movements. I'm caked in cuckoo spit and creepy-crawlies from pushing the branches back down. We balance on the hedgerow for hours, and I am taught patience more efficiently than by any sermon.

Gradually, more of the devout appear. A trickle at first,

then a pilgrimage of them, growing into a full-blown procession across the fields. They all say the same thing, looking at Dad and me perched up high on the perfect spot in the hedgerow, *early bird gets the worm*, and Dad would say *you'd have to get up pretty early to beat us alright*, and they'd laugh, and I do too, as if any part of our success has been my responsibility. I wonder how my Dad does that, talks to people like he knows them, puts them at ease, gets them laughing with just a few words. I wonder if I'll ever be that confident. I put my hands in my pockets and try to stand broad like him.

An excitement charges the air as the crowd grows, spreading out like crows on a telephone wire, then becoming two, three people thick, all of them craning their necks to see the road, an hour passing, maybe more. Someone further down the line has a wireless radio, and news of the premiership filters through the gathered, whispers of goals scored, shocking tackles, and a penalty that should have been, or shoulda-me-hole, depending who you heard it from.

There comes a sound then, a chorus of angels, rising through the trees. You know Dad has picked a good corner when you see the back end of the Ford first. Around the bend it comes, angled like a jet plane against a fierce wind, wheels spinning so much that the car seems bolted to the road for a moment, and through the window you can see the driver, only the eyes of him mind, the rest of his face lost inside his helmet, but you can tell from just his wide unblinking eyes, that he is on the limit, he has ascended, reached a higher plane of concentration and focus, and as he wrestles with the steering wheel, he is keeping the thing on the road with pure faith alone. And you understand then that god has made man, yes – but man has done one better with the MKII Escort. And just as soon, the car is gone – leaving behind vibrations in the earth, an incense of pure petrol, and an almighty shower of pebbles in its wake. And I turn away but Dad has me tucked in the wing of his jacket, hugging me close. We laugh, ears ringing, with mud-splattered faces.

*

On the way home, I play with dinky cars in the back seat, pushing them back and forth and blowing through my lips, trying to replicate the animal growl of that engine, and fighting sleep in the slow crawl of traffic. *First in, last out,* Dad says.

I think I remember him saying the same thing when we were late to Mass once. I drift off to water drops running down the windshield, glowing red in the trail of taillights, and the round-up of Sunday sport on the radio. The sleep is restless and car-sick, my head lolling this way and that, but when I wake up, my Dad is steady at the wheel.

What Casket

Tatora Mukushi

I had never heard of Emmett Till, then suddenly three different references in a week. I got curious and read up on him. He was just a kid. It was 1941, so I guess back then people named their kids 'Emmett'. I bet his parents didn't expect him to be famous. It's one of those names though. Like he could be a US senator or a jazz musician. A pioneer of something. Anything. Fuck, he didn't even see his fifteenth birthday.

*

The first time I heard his name, I was listening to an audiobook by a famous black death row lawyer. I was in the garden trying to DIY a sandpit, listening to him talk about innocent people spending decades of their lives in living hell, never mind those who died innocent. And I was moving dirt from one side of the garden to the other in a plastic bucket with my earphones in. It's all I can do to stay sane these days, and I'm imagining the kids will need it since they've shut everything down and there's nothing at all to do at their mum's. At least the manual labour's kept me from getting pot-bellied clearing my beer backlog. I won't go as far as to say that I have a gardener's tan but I'm not the pale fish of December. I'd have been on holiday twice by now. In fact, I probably would have listened to the same audiobook on a lilo in the hotel pool, heavily basted and trashed from the all-inclusive bar. Even if I'd been awake, I doubt I would have recalled his name. Especially not a name as weird as that.

You could imagine the story playing out as a TV mini-series. A couple of old detectives reminiscing about this case they broke despite the fact that no one they interviewed was willing to say a thing, even the kid's parents. It would get a rewrite though, so the parents turn out to be way more wealthy than anyone imagined, or his dad saved some guy in the war who turned out to be a big shot and so makes things happen behind the scenes. And it would end with someone learning a valuable lesson and we find out just how important that case was to the detectives' careers.

*

The second time I heard his name I was on a reunion video call with some old university friends, and someone mentioned visiting his memorial. I completely missed seeing it when Becca and I went to Mississippi. Or maybe it was that the tour guide didn't want to take us there, us being a mixed couple. It was obvious then because he'd asked us all where we were from. I don't think he had seen a black woman with a British accent before. He didn't say a word to her when he was asking me about Scotland and that damn *Outlander* show. She'd wandered off to find coffees, and when she came back, he gave her a weird look as if she was tagging on to our tour group, trying to get a freebie.

Anyway, somebody on the call who I hadn't seen for years asked me how she was and I had to explain the break-up all over again. Apparently, breaking up on a holiday is sensational and I'm a fool for doing it. Like I don't know that already. And apparently, there's no such thing as racist black families. I can never explain it without people telling me I'm playing the victim. Anyone who knew her called her 'Ms OCD' so it was easier to blame it on that. At least then I only caught a ribbing for being under the thumb. I could share the photos, the ones of the bruises that I saved just in case it ever became a he-said-she-said thing. Let the pictures tell a story. God, I hope no one is locked down with her for the duration. What a nightmare.

*

Someone pointed out that she only used to date white guys. How she boasted that she was too 'in your face' for black guys and how they expected women to be meek and servile, which wasn't for her. All of her pals were white too, which only made her stand out more, like this tall obsidian obelisk. I bet if I spoke to any of her exes they would all say the same thing —how she preached about empowerment and being on the right side of history. Like some kind of woke demon, fucking us into black consciousness.

She pirated American talk shows and we'd watch them

on her laptop over breakfast. I ditched most of them when we split, except one that I still keep up with. In one episode, they interviewed a congressman from Illinois. His mission was to erect a memorial to Emmett in Chicago because that's where he was from, even though he'd been lynched in Mississippi.

See, I was lying when I said I got curious. I broke. When I heard that congressman talking about him, I just started crying at the thought of this kid going to visit his aunt and uncle and winding up dead. Not just dead but the most horrific god-awful death you can imagine for anyone, let alone a kid. I used to go down to Troon every summer. At fourteen, I went on the coach myself, with my first iPod and Nike trainers. Imagine if a week later, my mum was deciding between an open or closed casket.

Quartet

Jon Russell Herring

1. COMMUNIQUÉS

Dear Jon,
As you leave school, we wish you all the best in your future career. Please consider staying in touch by joining the Old S▓▓▓▓▓▓ Association! You will receive our annual magazine.

Dear Jon,
We hope you enjoy the latest edition, which is enclosed. It's already five years since the class of 1988 left us! We will be hosting a barbecue on 3rd July this year at school – do come along and tell us what you have been up to since we last saw you!

Dear Jon,
We know that many ex-pupils live a long way from school and are unable to attend the annual barbecue. We would like to take this opportunity to let you know that in the coming days, a current sixth former will be calling you as part of our new telephone campaign to let all former

alumni know about the exciting new developments at school.

Dear Mr Herring,
Thank you for updating your delivery address for future editions of *Old S▓▓▓▓* magazine. We note that you have not provided a phone number at your new home. If this was in error, please use the enclosed postage-paid envelope to return the Alumni Details form. Thank you!

Dear Mr Herring,
We are pleased to inform you that the school now has an internet 'website' with a dedicated page for alumni. Many old members also have E-Mail addresses now – would you be happy to receive updates and the magazine electronically?

(Please note that we are still hoping to update all our alumni records with current phone numbers, and there is also the chance for you to inform us of your current household income on the new webpage.)

To: jon_herring@hotmail.com
Subject: 10 years!
We are delighted to report that we have begun a new funding drive for alumni bequests. We will be happy to share the details at your cohort's Ten-Year Anniversary Barbecue, or please click on the link below. There, you also have an opportunity to tell us about your current job and any family news!

Dear Dr Herring,
We are writing to you by 'snail mail' as our mail system shows that some of our recent email messages went undelivered.

Retirement news: as someone who studied Geography with us here in the 1980s, we are sad to inform you that Mr Derek Marshall is leaving us this summer after nearly forty years in the Humanities Department. Please join us at the annual barbecue to help bid Mr Marshall a fond farewell!

Dear Dr Herring,
We're sorry we didn't see you at the barbecue last summer. As the new president of the Old S▓▓▓▓▓▓, I write to tell you that we need your permission, under new GDPR regulations, to continue sending you updates. Please do also tick the relevant boxes so that we can tailor our newsletters to include information about the clubs and societies you belonged to at school.

Dear Dr Herring,
It feels like it is still a new feature of our landscape, but the school LGBTQ society celebrates its 7th birthday this autumn. We would love former students to share their experiences while at our school for the upcoming LGBT+ History Month project.

Dear Dr Herring,
We know we only recently contacted you about your school memories, but we would really love to include more stories

from our valued former students. To this end, we have set up an electronic submission form – scan the QR code below to participate!

2. MÉMOIRE

Welcome to the Share Your Story section of the school website! Please add your memories below.
[You have 2,500 characters remaining]

> *At school in the 1980s, 'gay' was thrown around a lot as an insult. It was a well-used currency and seemed to reap immense dividends for the boys (our school was co-ed then, but it was always the boys) who constantly used it to police other boys' behaviour.*
>
> *Along with all the other non-sporty kids, or the ones who liked learning and didn't dick around in lessons, I got used to being called gay, homo, bent, queer, shirt lifter, fudge packer, shit stabber, arse bandit, knob jockey – or just hearing John Inman noises (look him up) whenever I put my hand up in class.*
>
> *I was 13 years old in 1984. I was not out at school. In fact, I didn't even start to identify as a gay man until I was 16, and it took another three years for me to come out to my family. I had long since left school by then.*
>
> *There was one day that summer when the giggling and commotion in form 3K had a different quality to it. Subdued, almost hysterically stifled, and with a real sense of anticipation that something different was happening. In Geography, which I think was the second to last lesson of*

the day, my teacher Derek Marshall asked me to stay behind after the lesson. He reached over my shoulder and unpeeled a piece of A4 paper that was stuck to the back of my blazer with two pieces of masking tape.

'Jon, I'm very sorry about this. I decided it was better to remove it out of the sight of the others so as not to inflame the situation. I gather it has been there all day.'

I look at the paper. Time slows down. On it, in black marker pen, in all capital letters, is simply written AIDS CARRIER. Time stops.

I do not move. I look at the paper again. I look at Mr Marshall. His face is expressionless. He turns and drops the paper, intact, in his classroom bin. It is still face up, mocking me, threatening me, but all you can see now is AIDS CAR.

I say nothing. Derek Marshall says nothing. I wait for him to tell me that it's all going to be okay. That he will find the boy who has done this to me today and punish him. The silence and awkwardness stretch for another half minute or so. Nothing.

I pick up my black Puma canvas school bag, and walk out of the room.

And then 38 years later I was invited to a fucking barbecue?

[You have 281 characters remaining]

Please click 'Preview' to continue.
Thank you.

Here is how your text will look. We use DeepL technology to spellcheck and pre-scan your text.

Step One: please read the following suggested amendments to your entry:

    1. homo – did you mean 'home'?
    2. shit stabber – did you mean 'shirt stabber'?
    3. arse bandit – did you mean 'Clean Bandit'?
    4. fucking barbecue – did you mean 'duckling barbecue'?

To ignore the suggestions and proceed, click on 'Submit'.

Thank you.

Step Two: please do not leave this page while we are submitting your story.

Oops we've hit a problem! We were unable to accept some items in the text entered. Please check the error message below.

The following items have been flagged as offensive
by our systems:

AIDS CARRIER

3. RÉSUMÉ

I didn't click on Submit that day. (I did not submit to my rage.) As I was typing the story into the box, I started to wonder if it was a childish and pointless response. It reminded me of my behaviour in the early days of social media when I'd occasionally retweet something with a sneering put-down. Some person who knew nothing about my specialism in linguistics, who'd come out with a comment about dialects that barely disguised their classism.

I quickly learned the little adrenaline rush you get from being right and making others wrong in public. *I'll show them.* Over time I also learned that the satisfaction from doing this was short-lived and said more about me than it did about them. *That showed me.*

So why do I feel this hurt so acutely now, four decades later? I've been shamed in public many other times. Haven't we all? I buried it all within me, we bury it all within us and it helps make us who we are. And Section 28, which banned the promotion of gay and lesbian relationships by schools and local authorities – that became law in the UK a couple of years after AIDS CARRIER. But we organised and we fought, and Section 28 was repealed another fifteen years later in 2003. We did not submit.

*

I console myself that something like this could not happen to a 13-year-old now. I resolve to make a story out of it, a story or a poem. A triptych. Out of curiosity, I google "S▒▒▒▒ G▒▒▒▒ School LGBT History Month" and I find a podcast on Spotify from February 2022. It's by current sixth formers with their history teacher, Tim Long.

Here is my queer joy. Here is progress.

4. DÉNOUEMENT

Did I speak too soon?

2023. It feels like they're coming for us again. I think about how my story from 1984 has dated, or not; how in 1984 we had moral panics, but no one had used the words *culture war* yet. And then I consider whether I can – whether I should – whether it's *in my lane to* – write about the vigils this week for Brianna Ghey, a 16-year-old transgender girl murdered in a park in Culcheth, Cheshire. That's 18 miles from S▓▓▓ G▓▓▓ School in a straight line. What are the lines, straight or winding, that join my story to now?

And then, out of the blue:

> Alan McMunnigall is inviting you to a scheduled Zoom meeting
> Topic: Anthology?
> Time: Feb 21, 2023 02:00 PM London
> Join Zoom Meeting
> https://us04web.zoom.us/j/7247=theQRc0de@fewPag3sBackW0rks,btw-Try1t?
> Meeting ID: 724 3610 5060
> Passcode: 219EX4

```
Transcript of Zoom call by McGahan Transcriptions
Ltd. Thanks for your custom.
```

Alan: Hi Jon, new haircut? It's good to see you. This should only take five minutes, I reckon.

Jon: No, it was a nice surprise. It was a fun class again last week, by the way. Is that a new Dylan poster on your wall? So, yeah. The title on the invitation was. . .exciting?

Alan: Well, under the circumstances, I decided against asking you to stay behind after class. . .I'd like to put your piece in the anthology next year. What do you think?

Jon: Oh my God. You serious?

Alan: Absolutely.

Jon: I don't even need to think about it. Yes. Yes!

Alan: You've still got time to edit it and. . .

Jon: Yeah, oh. . .I'm not sure how brave I am in terms of. . .

Alan: It's fiction, Jon. You're in control, so. . .

Jon: Well, it's autofiction, yeah. Feel a bit pretentious saying that. So 'real' people might. . .they're gonna read it?! [Pause]. I love the paradox of claiming I didn't click send cause making it public might look like it's trying to settle old scores.

Alan: Mm-hmm.

Jon: And, it can't be a coincidence – I met my friend Julie last night, she was saying that with memoir, once it's out there, there's no taking it back. [Pause]. I don't know how the Geography teacher would feel, you know, it's. . .

Alan: Well, it's in your court.

Jon: I could change his name? Or make him Mr X or something? But no, um. . .No. I want it all to be true.

Alan: I wouldn't worry, Jon. There's more than one kind of truth. . .

Jon: OK. Let's do it.

Alan: I'll give you a deadline. Think about the title, too. It might turn into something other than a triptych? And see you in class on Sunday.

For Karen McLeod

For review/signature

Laura Givens

another one from the backlog – let me know if you want to discuss –

[MONTH XX, 2022]

Dear Mr Addams,

Thank you for your April 18, 2004 letter to President George W. Bush. Briefly, you requested that the President investigate a 'series of astral phenomena' which led to the apparent abduction of your spouse and adopted daughter by an 'awe-inspiring golden orb.'

Thank you as well for your correspondence dated April 29, 2004; May 31, 2004; December 25, 2004; June 9, 2007; August 11, 2010; August 23, 2010; September 12, 2011; April 18, 2017 and May 5, 2017.

Upon receipt, all materials were reviewed by the White House Office of Executive Correspondence and Outreach (WHOECO), which, in consideration of your concerns regarding:
- 'celestial bodies';
- 'possibly malignant. . .and almost violently intelligent forces. . .as yet unknown to man';

- 'moon emissions, solar flare transmissions'; and
- 'extra-intra-inter-stellar technologies',

forwarded your correspondence to the National Aeronautics and Space Administration (NASA).

NASA neither investigated nor failed to investigate your claims, and accordingly neither determined nor failed to determine the nature of the intelligences, emissions, transmissions, technologies, or other pertinent matters.

After which time, NASA forwarded your correspondence to the Environmental Protection Agency (EPA), Office of Environmental Emission and Air Events (OEEAE).

The OEEAE takes your concerns seriously, and having carefully reviewed your observations, records, claims, requests, and queries, now provides the following response:

- Regarding your allegation of water contamination of the Grand River and its tributaries, located in both Missouri and Iowa: The Grand River Watershed undergoes regular periodic testing for potential impurities, mineral content, salinity, and other environmental markers. Enclosed, please find the publicly available water quality data for Calendar Years 2008-2017.

- Regarding your request for Agency participation in efforts to locate missing persons: OEEAE offers its sincere wishes for the safe return of your loved ones, but cannot comment on, participate in, or interfere with the actions of law enforcement in this or any other matter.

- Regarding your request for explanation, clarity, and/or insight into the phenomena that you witnessed over the course of more than thirty years, from that first 'shard of blue light maybe indigo but bold and gentle at once' you saw over your home in Chillicothe, Missouri, February 9, 1997, to the subsequent 'burst of green yellow maybe what is called chartreuse, but iridescent, shimmering, like a Fourth of July sparkler' which 'came closer than [one] thought possible so that it had to touch [one] but [one] couldn't feel it not on [one's] skin but six layers deeper', and the much later 'storm. . .electric and raw. . .but even inside it. . .[you] could see the whole thing the way it was light but so much more, all colors, better than any rainbow, kind, and wholesome, and healthy, like a bike ride in June', which 'didn't seep into [you] but just sat on [your] skin, [yours] and Judy's and her little girl, Eliza's, [your] daughter no matter that [you weren't] hers by blood', and finally the

    all-encompassing awe-inspiring golden orb, pulsing, tacky, humid. . .alive and. . .pleasurable. . .so that [you, Judy, Eliza] in the light felt so happy, were laughing and couldn't stop and Judy said *oh honey it's just nothing like we thought it would be oh my* and little Eliza, only six, said *mommy daddy mommy daddy* just jumping and clapping her perfect hands like. . .Christmas morning. . .and the heavy, golden, orb-air coated [one's] throat, tasted sweet [so that one had to] wonder how [one] could even breathe but it was...perfection, and then Eliza said *daddy?* sounding only a little unsure, so [you] went to pick her up but before [you] could catch her Judy said *honey?* and grabbed [your] arm and when [you] turned to [Judy] she was already gone, but Eliza was still asking *daddy?* but [upon reflection you realize] she had already gone too, before Judy even, and then the light the orb the comfort the magnificence of love was gone, but [you] remember in [your] bones how glorious it was, even as [you] still hear Eliza saying *daddy?* still feel the tug of Judy's hand on [your] sleeve but they're both gone [five, ten, twenty-five] years now, how is it,

how is it that you were separated from them with no warning, and that subsequently, despite objections, wishes, thoughts and prayers, you continue to experience the as-yet ongoing 'series of astral phenomena.' How, moreover, you continue to 'enjoy it and take comfort in it even': OEEAE appreciates you bringing this matter to our attention. Unfortunately, despite NASA's unilateral decision to forward your correspondence to this Office, OEEAE lacks the capacity, authority, and will to offer you the guidance and support that you seek.

Recognizing the limited utility of this gesture, we have nevertheless enclosed contact information for a number of organizations that may be better able to assist you.
OEEAE now considers this matter closed. Further inquiries

should be directed to the EPA Midwest Regional District Office in Chicago, Illinois: http://www.EPA.District.chi4.gov/info_qry.

Sincerely,

[signature block]

Meg's Day Off

Maggie Reeve

Meg dried her hands on the tea towel and picked up the phone. It was Sheila from across the road.
  Are you alright to make sandwiches for me again?
  Yes, of course, Meg said. How many rounds? She caught sight of herself in the hall mirror and looked away.
  Two please, and don't forget to cut the crusts off.
  But that's such a waste.
  You know I can't bite through the crusts, said Sheila. You can buy loaves without crusts on now. Anyway, thanks, she said, and put the phone down.
  All these people at their wits' end with no money to feed their families, and Sheila thinks nothing of wasting food. Still, she's a poor soul, this is the least I can do.
  Meg picked up her lipstick and made her mouth into an O shape. She applied a layer of colour then put her lips together to spread it evenly. Not bright enough, just a wee bit more. She loved starting a new lipstick with its sloping, glossy end. It was a lovely new shade too. A change. She plumped her hair up with her fingers. Maybe a change of colour is needed here too, she thought, moving her head from side to side.

When the doorbell rang she was in the bathroom with her head in the sink. She grabbed a towel and wound it round her hair, ran down the stairs and saw a note on the doormat. She picked it up.

PARCEL IN GREENHOUSE, it said in thick black felt-tip pen. Why couldn't he wait till I got to the door, she thought. Suppose it's to do with not spreading the virus. She put the note on the hall table. I think I'll tell Sheila I'm not cutting the crusts off, or maybe I'll just say I forgot.

On her way back upstairs she saw a spider running into that crack she'd been meaning to fill for ages. She only remembered when she saw it. I'll have to put it on my list.

FILL CRACK ON STAIRS. No. FILL CRACK IN WALL.

Her hair was dry now and she applied more lipstick and a touch of blusher before going out to the greenhouse for the parcel. Just because you're self-isolating doesn't mean you can let yourself go. As she went up the garden she remembered Sheila hadn't said what she'd like in her sandwiches. I'll grate some cheese and open a tin of tuna. She says she likes salad cream mixed with tuna, keeps it moist.

Years ago she was sent on a self-assertiveness course, of all things. It was rubbish, all she could recall was being told to say **NO** if someone asked to borrow money. How cruel. I'm being assertive now, she thought, opening the greenhouse door. I'm doing something now, instead of putting it off. I've decided to do it and I'm doing it. She propped the door open, and tripped over the step. Bloody thing, why did they have to have a step into a greenhouse? The package was resting against the staging where she was growing tomatoes, but they were still green. Before she picked it up she watered a few things and went back to the house, got scissors out of the drawer and opened it. It was a battery for the window cleaning thing she bought four years ago and never used. This could have come in a much smaller box. She folded it up for recycling, remembering the programme she'd watched with all these people scooting around on wheels, picking and packing everything at great speed. What an exhausting job, you couldn't work till you're seventy doing that.

The cat rubbed himself against her leg.

Are you hungry? she said.

Miaow.

I'll give you something, but don't eat it all at once.

The cat ate some and left the rest. He jumped up and sat on the windowsill where he found a fly to play with.

Meg grated some cheese, mixed it into the tuna and added salad cream. She dipped her finger in it. Sheila will love that. She made the sandwiches up, cut the crusts off, sliced them into little triangles and arranged them in a plastic box. There was a bag of six packets of Salt & Shake crisps in the cupboard. Sheila would probably like a few of these, so she put a packet on top of the sandwich box, checked her lipstick in the hall mirror and walked across the street. There was a stool outside Sheila's door. After ringing the bell she put the box and the crisps on it, so Sheila wouldn't have to bend down too far. Before she returned to her own house, she peeped through Sheila's window and saw her getting out of her chair. She's heard me, she thought, and went back across the street. Just before opening her door she looked back. Sheila was picking up her delivery and waving. She mouthed a big THANK YOU and blew a kiss.

A Swear Jar for Saint Joseph

Matthew David Scott

John stands over the prone electrician. He displays no sense of urgency. Simon hopes that he is just trying to keep the men calm; moments ago, as they'd all gathered for toolbox talk, there had been a flash and a bang and the electrician had ended up where he is now. Everyone looks at John. John looks at the electrician's left foot. He spots a white scuff on the newly laid floor.

'Where's that stupid cunt?' he says. The junior labourer appears from behind a bundle of architrave.

'What have I told you about dragging the plasterboard? Fucking state of that.'

Now he spots a dry-lining lad with his phone out.

'Put it away, tricky bollocks,' he tells him, and the dry-lining lad puts it away. 'Never fucking off the things.' John takes a bookie's pen from behind his right ear.

Simon steps forward.

'Shit. . John, I'm going to have to ring an ambulance.'

John rails a fence of tallies on the back of his hand. Ruth's name still bleeds into the creases of his knuckles. He drops down to a knee and reaches for the electrician's foot.

'No!' shouts Simon. 'He might still be live.'

'Well, if he's dead,' John says, rising to his feet, 'I'm having his boots.'

The electrician rolls onto his back. He can't keep up the joke any longer. The laughter gushes, its torrent taking the other men with it. Even John is smiling. Simon shakes his head at being had and smiles too. He gets back to the toolbox talk.

'Right,' he says, unlocking the iPad. 'The safe use of steps and ladders.'

*

It's Lent but looks like November. A storm is supposed to be blowing in that night. John and Simon walk across the forecourt. The canopy is already up but concrete is yet to be poured. Two large holes gape in the ground by a JCB.

'I dug the pits myself. Tanks go in next week,' says John.

'Looking good,' says Simon. He's had to park his Land Rover on the main road. He worries about his bike fixed to the back.

The cabin shakes as they step inside. The walls are blank. There's a prickly blue carpet, a desk and a filing cabinet. On the desk, an empty two-litre Coke bottle is cut at the shoulders and half-filled with change. Other stacks of shrapnel are arranged around it like cairns. John moves a few and then heads to the filing cabinet. On the top is a kettle. He switches the kettle on and then opens one of the drawers. He takes out two mugs and a jar of instant coffee, sits, and licks a thumb before starting to rub out the tallies on his hand.

Simon has been sitting this whole time. His six-foot-odd is folded up into a small orange chair.

'So, John,' he says, 'anything we discuss today. . .'

TSCHH!

'I mean, it goes without saying that—'

TSCHH!

'Can you?—'

John stops dropping the coins into the bottle. He's known what's coming for months.

'It's my swear jar,' he says, and he tilts the bottle forward towards Simon. 'You said shit in the shop. And bastards.'

'I never said bastards,' says Simon.

'Cough up, you perishing twat,' says John. 'It's for St Joseph's Penny.'

Simon attempts to tap his pockets.

'I haven't got any cash on me,' he says. 'How about we go for a pint after work and. . .'

'Sugar?' says John, fetching the kettle.

'No. Thanks,' says Simon.

'I've got sweeteners?'

Simon shakes his head. He realises he's still wearing his hardhat. He takes it off and begins to run the rim through his fingers.

'It's genetic anyway. The type I've got.'

John pours two black coffees. It was the diabetes that got Ruth in the end. Simon drops the hardhat into his lap and takes the coffee from John with both hands. He wonders how full that swear jar is going to be by the end of this conversation.

*

The place Simon has picked to die might not seem particularly beautiful; the tide pulls the brown water back from the banks, and empty cans of lager spawn in the slosh. He begins another lap, checks his progress on the phone attached to his handlebars. He hasn't yet found a place to slip in.

*

John always has a bolthole when working away. Off site, he can't be with the rest of them, especially Simon. He feels bad for the guy but no matter how many times John tells him that he was never the alcoholic. . .well, it's difficult enough to not think of Ruth with every clenched fist. So, John keeps things like this to himself: it's the oldest pub in the town, hidden between bars that flex and palpitate with growth hormone and cheap cocaine. Up around the walls are etchings of radicals, prints of pamphlets and manifestos. He stands and wanders over to a small library of donated books on four or five shelves. He's not earned a conversation with the landlord yet but is on nodding terms. He looks along the spines. He hasn't finished a book since he left her at the hospital that last time. He remembers the amount of space in the bed when he climbed in with her, the machines silent. He remembers the weight of her as he held on, almost nothing. He grabs a book, black, the spine forked with white creases. He goes back to his table and puts it there, next to the mobile phone Simon bought him.

*

A blue blob tracks the red line of Simon's ride, his final moments sucked up into real-time data, waiting to be spat out across social media. The wheels of the bike sound like a jackhammer on the footbridge. Lovers' padlocks are closed around safety wires. He thinks of his wife. He's well insured but it has to look right. He thinks of his children, both grown now. They love him but none of them need him. If they still did, would that change anything, he wonders? Would he have felt anger rather than fear when the debt collectors turned up? Would he have chased them off in protective fury like his old man instead of sobbing as he bowed his long body beneath the bay window? Simon is not his father. He is not the tough man that built this firm from nothing. Simon is just a blue blob about to depart from a red line and disappear into a brown river. It begins to rain, and a message rolls down the screen of his phone.

*

It's morning. The junior labourer is on duty to scrub the Portaloo. Beige water flecks his boots and the bottom of his joggers. He stands with a bucket, waiting for the men to finish. They laugh as they tag-team for hungover shits. In the bucket, bleach clouds rise into a swirl, and all the junior labourer wants to do is vomit. John looks over and smiles to himself; he sees a car begin to pull onto the site.

'Whoa!' John waves his arms and walks towards the site entrance. The car stops. It's a taxi, and he puts his hand on the roof at the driver's side as the window buzzes down. John offers an arm to the forecourt.

'It's like a swamp, mate, any further and you'll be stuck.'

The taxi driver tosses his head back.

'Where do you want me to drop this then?'

John peers in at the passenger in the back.

'Fucking hell,' he says, 'We better get out the first aid kit.'

*

John plops a Solpadeine into a glass of water. Simon flinches in the orange chair.

'Thought you were going home this morning?' says John.

Simon stands, squinting.

'Wanted to check for storm damage. Might be a claim.'

John passes him the fizzing glass.

'I can have the lad do it when he's finished with the shitter.'

'Prefer to take a look myself,' says Simon.

John runs a finger across the sliced rim of the swear jar. He watches Simon down the cloudy water. Simon looks awful. He catches a burp in his fist.

'Not in fucking here,' says John.

'I'm fine, I'm fine,' says Simon. 'I'll be fine.' He is wearing the same clothes he wore yesterday. He thinks for a second or two of thanking John for last night.

'Better go and see what I can find,' he says instead.

John pushes the door shut and goes to sit at his desk. He closes his eyes and knits his hands over his belly. He remembers the day Ruth shat all over the flat. She was in the chair mostly by then, one leg gone, so he thought he could count on her not getting hold of any booze while he was out. By the time he'd got back from work there was an empty bottle of brandy on the floor, and she'd shat everywhere trying to get to the toilet on her crutches.

He opens his eyes and stands up. He goes over to the filing cabinet and opens a drawer. Inside is a box of bookie's pens, some drawings and the book from the pub. He takes out the book and is about to start reading when—BangBangBang!

He goes over and opens the door. The junior labourer is standing, slightly out of breath.

*

They walk quickly to the canopy. The junior labourer is explaining what he heard and saw.

'Fucking shook the whole thing,' he says.

The bottom of a ladder is sunk into the wet ground, the top of it resting against the edge of the canopy.

'Did you go up and check on him?' John says. The junior labourer looks down at his boots.

'It's alright,' says John, and he goes to grab the ladder but realises he's still holding the book. He walks over to the JCB and chucks the book in the cab. As he turns back to the canopy, he notices that the other men on the site have begun to come out to see what is happening. He puts a foot on the second rung of the ladder and looks out at them.

'Any danger one of you might ring an ambulance?' He begins to step up. 'Just tell them not to come onto the site,' he shouts, 'they'll never get off.' He looks down at the junior labourer.

'Keep this thing fucking steady.'

As an apprentice, John's wedding ring had once caught on a scaffold clamp, snagging him in mid-stride and almost throwing him clean off the side of a block of flats. He'd taken the ring off that day and never wore it again, tattooing Ruth's name on his knuckles instead. He sees white bone beneath the greenish ink as he grips the ladder, finally reaching the top and clambering onto the flimsy canopy. He crawls his way over to Simon. He checks for a pulse and puts him in the recovery position. There doesn't seem to be any damage to the canopy. When he climbs back down, he tells the junior labourer to get up there; he tells him what the plan is.

*

John pulls himself into the cab of the JCB. He fires up the machine and manoeuvres it to where he can see the junior labourer's hardhat above the lip of the canopy, yellow against a clear, blue sky. He drops the bucket to pour out any rainwater, then extends the arm up towards the yellow.

The junior labourer shoves Simon's body towards the canopy's edge. He guides the bucket in with hand signals, John nudging the machine to exactly where it needs to be. A flat palm and the bucket judders. The junior labourer whispers and rolls Simon over the edge. John feels the weight in the bucket rock the cab. He brings him down gently.

[On a day]

David Harrison Horton

[Mid September's]

David Harrison Horton

Suffocation

Megha Shah

My best friend stopped talking to me last week. She walked into class, sat beside someone we both dislike and didn't look my way until I texted her multiple GIFs of Dwayne Johnson's raised eyebrow. There are things, she told me later, that she needed to address. I shrugged and she launched into a detailed analysis of our friendship – she found it difficult to find a common moral ground between us, it was becoming harder for her to ignore my opinionated proclamations about equality (whatever those were, I still don't know) and she felt suffocated by my feminism. She wanted to work towards our friendship, really, but I sometimes made her feel a little strangulated, you know what I mean?

There is a her-shaped hole in my social life now, and every time I look at a crow I resist the urge to tell her about it. I lock away inside jokes and memories too fresh to forget about when I realise I still haven't wrapped her birthday present. I put away the cadmium blue scarf, along with some other trinkets I don't want to see anytime soon, and choke on the hollowness of typing a perfunctory birthday message (with two exclamation marks and a single emoji) that will earn me a sad little reply in the next few hours. Nothing much has changed. I sit with new people in class and bring up generic, safe topics of conversation. We look at each other and nod and that's that.

Pills 'n' Thrills and Bellyaches

Sean McMenemy

In memory of Ryan

We were sitting on the dunny wall trying to finish the last of our cider when they appeared. The older team normally would just give you the nod and keep walking. That day though, they stopped and joined us. It was only me and Thomson left. Thomson himsel was older, maybe three or four years older than me, but he looked young, acted young, and always hung around wae the young team. He wisni interested in pubs and clubs. Aw he ever wanted to do was hang around the streets and drink and fight and wind folk up. Some of the older wans had started calling him Peter Pan.

When the conversation turned to a certain nightclub Thomson jumped right in. He was claiming he knew the heid bouncer and was convinced he could get me in. Said if they were aw going we should go too.

You're saying yer gaun tae get him into Flaunt? one of them said, pointing at me and laughing.

Cunt looks aboot twelve. Nae offence wee man, but you'd be lucky to get into the amusements at the Cross.

He was right. I was only fifteen. Old enough for a milk run maybe. I was lucky to be getting into the unders at Archaos, never mind the overs. Thomson was convinced though and dying to prove a point. He was always dying to prove a point to anybody that would listen.

Bet ye any money, he was shouting. Any fuckin money I'll get him in.

Thomson was the best liar I'd ever met. It was hard to tell what was the truth and what wisni sometimes, he was that sharp. Jackanory was another name of his.

Think you've been away in Neverland too long, one of them said.

Thomson was up aff the wall now and pacing up and doon. He hated when people didn't believe him. When he got angry he'd grit his teeth and clench and unclench his fists. It was good value watching him, he went on as if he'd never told a lie. Maybe in his own heid he hadn't.

We'll see about that. Come on Davie Boy, let's go, he said.

See ye in the dancing later Davie Boy.

Aye. Mind and bring yer Faither's wallet wae ye wee man. Drinks are oan you thinight, another one said.

Nae bother, I shouted back laughing.

Whit ye laughing at, Thomson said, when we turned the corner.

Them. Yer no actually serious. Ur ye?

Course I am. Think I'd make something like that up? We're fuckin gaun there thinight Davie Boy. Me and you in the dancin, taking aw their fuckin birds aff thum.

I donno mate, I said. I've no even got anything tae wear.

I'll kit ye oot. You'll be the best dressed cunt in there.

When we turned onto the main road he started running for a bus.

Come on, he shouted back at me.

I wisni up for it at all. But the thought of going home to sit in front of the telly wae ma maw and da was worse.

Thomson stayed in Foxbar, away on the other side of Paisley. The bus had to go through the toon to get there and that's where aw the Shortroods boys hung aboot. They were the gang we fought wae the most. The Paka they were called and we were the Ganja Derry. I always thought we had the best name oot ae aw the gangs. Druggy and Irish. I liked tae say we wur the dope-smoking freedom fighters. We used tae spray-paint hash leafs everywhere and write Y.G.D in between the stems. It looked cool as fuck. The only other way to get tae Thomson's was tae walk away up through the west end and it wisnae much safer there for him either. He was wanted aw over the toon for being a wido. There weren't many folk he hudnae pissed aff or wound up over the years. Seedhill was his only refuge noo and the poor cunt didnae even live there.

It was one of they old buses that stank, vibrated and jerked about like fuck. The driver didnae help matters wae his braking, it was like minor whiplash every few seconds.

That cunt driving the bus wae calipers on his feet? Thomson said.

Either that or he's got some size a stane in his shoe.

Haw, driver, lay aff the fuckin brakes, he shouted.

I saw him glancing back in his mirror and shaking his heid.

Some coupon on him, Thomson said.

Ribena face. Probably halfcut.

Should I ask him if he wants the last of ma cider, he said, taking a big swig.

That fuckin bottle's never-ending.

That made him laugh and he nearly choked on the stuff.

Yer right, he said, wiping the drink aff his face. Three litres is too much gut-rot for any man.

When the bus turned onto High Street we stopped at the lights. A crowd of boys appeared oot the Job Centre. Thomson turned in his seat and stuck his heid doon.

Fuck, he said. Don't look.

Where, I said.

Fuckin right there. It's them.

Who's them?

Shauny and Kev and Bruno and Quinny. The lotta them.

Next thing I heard was a bang at the window. You're deid, they were aw shouting. Two of them ran round the other side of the bus. Thomson jumped oot his seat and grabbed a hold of the back door that they were trying to pull open. The other two were pointing at me and running their finger doon the side of their face. They looked even bigger than I thought. I froze for a second, then managed to force myself up and run doon the front of the bus.

Fucking drive will ye, I shouted.

The two of them were trying tae force the front doors open. Just as one of them pressed the emergency button and the doors swung open, the lights changed and the driver sped off. His big foot had come in handy.

Cheers for that, I said to the driver. Fuckin saved us bigtime there.

Thomson was jumping aboot like a mad man, given them the finger oot the back windae. He lived for these kinda moments. Somehow he always managed tae get away, like some great escape artist. It was normally his speed that saved him. Called himself The Cheetah, really he was more like a gazelle. They were all desperate tae give him a doin and he loved winding them up aboot how they couldnae catch him. I didnae want to be there when they finally did.

They'll never fucking get me Davie Boy, he was shouting. Never. Never. Never.

*

His maw was always happy to see ye.

How you doing son? she said and hugged me as I came in the door.

She'd brought him up on her own and spoiled him rotten. Was nothing he didnae have. I donno how she done it, must've owed all sorts tae the catalogues.

No too bad Maggie, yoursel?

Quiet son. Apart fae running aboot after this yin, she said, giving him a kiss.

Ye'll never believe it Maw, he said. Aw the Paka nearly hud us oan the bus there. Didn't they Davie?

Aye, it was close.

What've ah telt ye aboot getting that bus, she said. Especially at the weekends, ye know they're always hingin aboot up that toon. Phone me next time and I'll get ye a taxi.

You'll need to get us wan back, he said. I'm taking the wee man dancin thinight.

Up Glesga?

Naw Paisley.

For god sake, she said. Have ye no learnt anythin after thiday?

It'll be fine, he said. Auntie Angie's man's the bouncer and aw the older wans are gaun.

Just be careful, she said walking intae the living room. And ye better no leave that boy on his ain, she shouted.

I started to get excited when Thomson opened his wardrobe. He'd good style and it was aw designer stuff. Everything was hung and neatly folded. I picked oot a Lacoste jumper I'd always loved.

What aboot this, I said.

That'll be right, I'm wearing that.

Uch come on, I said, pulling it oan. Looks good oan me.

He turned and saw me admiring it in the mirror. So it does, ya wee dick, he said laughing. If ye fuckin spill anything oan it yer paying fur it. I got that in Paris.

He'd never been tae Paris but I wisnae going to say anything and ruin ma chance. We were both mad intae claes and had swapped loads of stuff over the years. Was no way he'd have let anyone else wear that jumper but he knew how much I liked it.

Cheers, I said. What dae ye think would go wae it?

He picked oot a nice pair of shoes, jeans, and a polo.

Here, he said. Don't say I'm no good tae ye.

The outfit was proper gallus and when I stuck it oan I suddenly felt right up for it. Any booze in here? I asked.

Naw. I'll see if ma maw's got anything.

He returned wae a half bottle of vodka and Vimto for the mix.

Cheeky enough, he said.

I was halfcut by the time we were about to leave.

Let's get a look at you before ye go, Maggie shouted fae the living room.

Her and her pal were sat opposite each other smoking. Ye didnae want to be there too long or ye'd come oot stinking.

You'll be fighting them aff thinight Davie Boy, she said. Look at him Jeany, ain't he handsome. Wee Jeany was in the middle of putting oot a fag and lightin another. Aye, she said in between puffs. Handsome awright.

That's cause he's wearing ma claes, Thomson said, coming in at ma back.

Look better oan me than they dae you, I said.

You tell him son, Maggie said, laughing.

Time to go, Thomson said. Taxi's there.

*

We bumped intae Harrigan when we got out. Everyone's already inside, he told us.

Where've you been? Thomson asked.

Picking up the jack n jills.

This is gaun tae be some fuckin night, he said rubbing his hauns.

We joined the queue and I positioned myself on the inside. Thomson and Harrigan stood on my outer. I couldnae make oot what they were saying. Just kept my eyes fixed on the slabs, hoping naebody would notice me. The closer we got to the front the faster my heart went. Just as well I had Thomson's big jaiket oan or else everyone would've seen the state I was getting intae. Aw the drink had somehow worn off and any bravado I had in the taxi doon was well and truly gone. Ma laces had come undone and every time we shuffled up the line I thought I was going to trip. It was mad the way it happened, like something oot a movie. When we got to the barrier the bouncer unclipped the rope, slipped Thomson the passes and herded us through the door wae his big arm. Not a word was said and the next thing I knew I was running up the stairs after Harrigan. There was a couple in front of us paying at the booth. Thomson ran up at our backs and put his arm aroon ma shoulder. I turned and grabbed him and the two of us jumped up and doon together laughing.

What did I tell ye wee man, he was shouting in my ear. What did I fuckin tell ye. The Tomahawk Kid comes up trumps. Never doubt The Kid wee man, never doubt The Kid.

Calm it yous two or we'll end up getting tossed oot afore we even get fuckin in, Harrigan said.

Harrigan was older but still liked hanging wae us sometimes. He'd this mad stoned look aboot him. Wouldnae think he wis much of a fighter but he wis. He wis also now known as The Feg, cause he'd moved oota Seedhill into Feegie. I never called him it, but I found it funny how much he hated it.

Shut up Harrigan, Thomson said. We're untouchable in here. He wis holding up the passes and dancing on one foot.

You're delusional ya cunt, Harrigan said and grabbed them oot his hand.

Thomson nearly fell doon the stairs, managed to grab hold of the banister.

Give us wan, I said, putting ma hand oot.

Here, he said and handed them back. Just calm it.

Thomson got in first and ran ahead. He'd gathered the older wans together and when they saw me coming they aw started cheering. Felt as if I wis a celebrity, everyone shaking my haun, offering tae buy me a drink. It was a sweaty wee club, low ceilings, smoky and mobbed. They'd managed to get two tables together and everyone was standing roon them. I couldnae stop laughing at Thomson, he looked mair buzzin than me, jumping aboot and shouting his mouth aff to everybody. Even the older wans found it funny.

Best dressed cunt in here, he wis saying and pointing at me.

Big Bernie came over and handed me a beer. There ye go wee man, he said.

Cheers, I said and turned away.

I wis always that intimidated by the older wans and never knew whit tae say. It wis the mad unpredictability of them I couldnae get used tae. I never saw mysel as a fighter. Never pretended I wis either. I wis just in it for the patter, patter and the bevy, and the birds of course. I wis really hoping tonight to get ma first one over the line. There were plenty of them up on the dance floor. Chances looked good, odds were favourable, no like the fuckin school discos. I took a drink of beer and started to loosen up. DJ was playing some cracking tunes and I felt mysel moving tae the beat.

A few drinks later and me and Thomson were up oan the dance floor. I'd ma eye on this wee blonde bird that wis prancing aboot. Her pal and her kept dancing intae us and laughing. Thomson was pulling mad faces behind their backs and mouthing something I couldni make oot. I felt a hand on ma shoulder and turned to see Harrigan. He grabbed me by the face and kissed me oan the cheek. His eyes were huge and he was chewing fuck oota piece of gum. I'm sure he said I love you but I wisnae sure. Thomson was over next and three of us were in a huddle on the dance floor. Harrigan pulled out what looked like a wee bag of sweets.

Whit are they, I asked.

Ferraris, he said. And handed two to Thomson who swallowed them back.

But whit ur they?

Eccies, he said.

Awright. Any good?

Dynamite. Ye want a couple?

Donno man. Never taken them.

Just take wan, he said and put it in ma haun.

Will I be awright?

Aye. Yer wae us, int ye? he said.

I held it up to examine it. Wis a wee triangular yella thing wae a horse stamped in the middle. Looked like something ye'd get oot a penny mix. Surely it couldnae be that bad.

Get it doon ye, Thomson shouted and handed me his drink.

I hesitated a bit and they both gave us a look, so I swiftly gubbed it, washed it doon wae Thomson's drink. It left a rotten taste, bitter, like hairspray or something. I felt ma face screwing up.

Did ye get it doon? Thomson said.

Aye man. Stinking though.

Two of them laughed. Wee man's first eccie, Harrigan said.

Ferraris anol, Thomson said. Ye'll be flying.

Come oan I'll get us another drink, Harrigan said.

I'd almost forgot I'd taken anything after a while. We stood at the bar drinking for ages, talking about what would happen if the Paka came in. I didnae feel anything until Thomson pulled me up on the dance floor. That tune he always played wis oan but it sounded different. It wis so clear I could hear how it aw came together. The fuzz of the drum and bass went right through me. Thomson grabbed ma shirt and the two of us started bouncing aboot. It wis then I felt the rush. It wis instant. Like the buzz ye get when yer team scores in the last minute. The smile on my face wis getting wider and wider as waves of it kept coming.

Some dunt int it? Thomson said.

Unreal mate. Feel like I'm fuckin flying.

That's cause ye ur, he said. Bet ye never thought ye could feel this good?

There ain't no party like a Seedhill party, he shouted.

We're the Ganja Derry, I shouted back.

I'd nearly danced the heels aff Thomson's shoes before I went back tae the bar. Sweat wis pouring off me but ma mooth was dry as anything. I thought I was going tae pass oot fae the heat. I noticed the blonde lassie at the front of the queue. I pushed ma way in and tapped her oan the shoulder.

Do us a favour and get us a pint of water, I said.

She nodded and smiled. I stood under the aircon at the side of the bar to cool down. For some reason I couldnae stop grinding ma teeth and ma jaw was starting to hurt. I noticed the older wans were all up jigging now, they aw danced in the same tense way. Like boxers in the ring before the bell. Was funny watching them.

You just standing there or you going to help me, she shouted, holding out a load of drinks.

Aye, sorry.

Over to them, will ye, she said and pointed to a group of lassies at the far side. It was like an obstacle course getting through the crowd withoot spilling them. I put them on the table and ran back tae find her waiting beside the bar.

Here's your water, she said.

Cheers, I said and gulped it doon.

She looked even more stunning in the light. Her skin was golden and her eyes were like big lagoons. Everything aboot her was just perfect.

Looks like you needed that, she said laughing. You need water when you're on pills.

How'd you know I'm on pills?

Your eyes and jaw are a bit of a giveaway.

Aye. Do I really look that bad?

Nah you're alright, she said and pushed her hair back. We're all on them too – got them off your pal over there. Think everyone in here's on them.

Brilliant, aren't they?

Yeah. Best ones I've had in ages, she said and took a drink.

Some guys beside us were trying to barge their way into the bar. One of them fell back, knocked the glass out her hand, and sent her flying forward. I managed to catch her before she fell down the stairs.

You alright? I said, lifting her up.

Yeah, she said, wiping the drink off her dress.

Sorry, the big guy shouted over.

Aye ye will be, I said. Loud enough for her to hear but no him.

I don't think he meant it, she said. Just as well you caught me.

Couldnae have ye taking a heider onto the dance floor.

She was still holding onto my arm and for some reason I couldni decide whit tae do. We both stalled for a moment and then turned to kiss each other at the same time. She had this mad gloss on her lips that tasted like cherry. I think I would've kissed her forever if Thomson hidnae came over.

I'm sorry for interrupting, he said and pulled my shirt. But I need to ask my good friend here something. He put his arm round me and turned me away.

You don't mind dae ye? he said to her with a smile.

Whit the fuck man? Can you no see I'm in the middle a something?

Calm doon. She's no gaun tae run away.

Seriously man, whit is it?

See her pal that wis dancin wae us earlier.

Aye.

Her sitting over there, he said and pointed to the table I'd taken the drinks to.

Whit aboot her?

Well I've been waiting for her tae come back up and dance but I don't think she's gaun tae.

So whit do ye want me to dae aboot that?

Well, since it's your wee bird's pal, I was thinking you could get her tae introduce us.

How'd you no just go over yersel?

Cause she's sitting wae company.

Whit difference does that make?

A big difference. Look ye gaun tae do me the favour or no?

I've just started.

Don't forget the only reason you're kissing her is cause of me.

He was starting to get angry, daein that thing wae his hauns, thing he does when folk don't believe him. I couldnae exactly say naw.

I'll see what she says.

That's it, he said.

She was touching her hair and smiling when I got back over to her.

He likes Jen, doesn't he? she said.

How'd you know?

They've been eyeing each other up all night. She's into him too but she'll never make a move.

He's wanting to know if you'll introduce him?

Suppose so. I'm always doing this kinda thing for her. Let's go over then.

Wait a minute. You've no even told me your name yet.

My name?

Aye. Surely I should know that first.

She laughed and kissed me on the cheek. It's Laura, she said.

Laura, that's nice. I'm Davie. Ma pals call me Davie Boy but you can call me whatever ye want. I'm no fussy that way.

Davie Boy, she said. That's funny.

*

Once Thomson was introduced he wis quickly holding court and cracking jokes. After a while the others left and it was just the four of us. We were getting on that well it felt like we'd known each other for years. Had me thinking this could be the start of something. Four of us going on double dates together, fancy restaurants, proper pubs, maybe even weekends away. They looked the type for that. Wurnae the kind you'd find roon the back of the Lagoon drinkin Pulse. Naw they wur the proper classy burds. No the kind we wur used tae.

Another round, Thomson was shouting and holding up his pint.

If ye don't mind, I said.

It's your shout ya cunt.

I couldnae remember if it wis or it wisnae and I couldnae be bothered getting intae wan aboot it wae him cause I'd never win.

What yous after girls? I asked.

Nothing, Laura said. We're just going to the toilet and then going to head back to Jen's. Why don't yous get your jackets and meet us outside.

Whit did I tell ye Davie Boy, Thomson kept saying as we waited for oor jaikets. Come oot wae me and you'll always get a burd.

I was going to point oot that it was me who actually got him sorted, but I just left it. Was better to keep it for later. Cast it up when everybody was there to hear it.

Have I done ye proud or have I done ye proud? he said, flicking his hand over the outfit.

*

Outside the stars were pure bright and the big moon hung over the Institute building. There was a loud hum fae the street lights and it felt like electricity was in the air. It was cold and I kept getting these wild shivers through me. Ma teeth were chattering and all I could smell was the fat fae the takeaway. The idea of eating made me feel sick. There was a few folk staggering aboot the lane. Like zombies oota the 'Thriller' video. I took a seat in the bus stop and rubbed ma hauns thigether for a heat.

Fuck. Don't look, Thomson said, sitting doon next to me. Harrigan's over there.

He was lying wae his back on the bonnet of a motor, arms oot like a starfish, looking up at the stars. Sounded like he wis laughing and talking to himsel but I couldnae make oot whit he was saying.

He's a fucking casualty thinight, Thomson said. Canny huv him ruining this for us.

I'd never seen Harrigan like that afore and I was quite worried, but no worried enough to put the rest of the night at risk. Think he'll be awright, I says.

Aye, fuck sake, it's Harrigan.

The girls appeared and walked out into the street laughing. I noticed a few older wans coming oot the takeaway across the road. Thomson shot up and diverted them roon the bus shelter and back towards the lane.

If we head this way ma uncle will pick us up in his taxi, he said.

I wisnae aware of any uncle wae a taxi but he managed tae convince me tae. All I could think aboot noo was the warm back seat of a Vectra. Ma hopes were dashed halfway up the lane when he turned roon and gave us his classic wink. I think he could've telt the lassies anything tae be honest. They wur away in a wee world ae their ain: whispering and giggling and falling intae each other. We wur lucky, when we got roon tae George Street a black hack appeared, and I managed tae flag it doon.

Right this way, I said sliding open the back door. Uncle Hackney has arrived.

Jen stayed in the tenements roon the corner fae Thomson's maw's hoose. Her flat was nice and warm. Was very similar tae ma auntie's place, big high ceilings, bay windows, and the vintage furniture. She'd loads of cool film and music posters on the walls. Some of the bands I knew and liked but there were others I'd never heard of. She had this great big sound system, booze everywhere, and a pile of weed on the coffee table.

Thomson was doing his usual, walking around inspecting everything. I sat doon on the sofa beside Laura. She put her arm round me, pulled me into her, and gave me a kiss. It felt like the two of us were melting intae one another.

This is some gaff you've got, Thomson said, looking through her CD collection.

Thanks, she said. Why don't you put something on?

You no got any dance stuff? he said, flicking through them like mad.

Dance stuff? She walked over and handed me and Laura a drink. This is the closest I've got to that, she said, and put a CD in. The music woke me up and it wisnae long before the three of us were dancing aboot the living room.

Whit is this? I asked Laura.

What?

The music.

It's the Happy Mondays. Do you like them?

They're fuckin brilliant!

I know, she said and pointed to this cool coloured poster on the wall that spelt out the name.

We drank and danced and danced and drank until the sun started coming up. When Jen pulled the thick curtains shut and put on the lamp the room glowed. I took a few draws of the joint that was being passed around, but I didnae really feel anything. I was still pretty wired when Thomson and Jen left us and went into the bedroom. My heart felt like it was gaun tae jump oot ma chest and I was sitting wae ma hand over it.

You alright, Laura said.

Aye, just feel a bit weird. Ye know?

Just try and relax, she said. You're just coming down, it's normal.

I tanned the rest of ma beer and went to grab Thomson's leftovers.

Take some water instead, she said, and handed me her glass.

I really wanted the beer but I took it just tae be nice.

Come over here, she said, and adjusted the cushions on the couch.

When we started kissing I calmed doon and the paranoia lessened. We were kissing for ages and it was that good I never thought aboot anything else. Wisnae until she started pulling ma belt aff that I moved ma hand up her skirt. We were fooling aroon for ages and it was great but when we got doon tae it I couldnae get it up.

Relax, she kept saying but every time she said it, it just made it worse. Aw I could think aboot was ma floppy disk. Floppy disk was the nickname ma pal got for ma problem noo. I donno how many times we tried but it felt like hunners. It was brutal. In the end I was that scunnered I couldnae even look at her anymair. It was a relief when she finally fell asleep cause I had nothing left tae say. I moved over tae the other couch and lit up a fag. I couldnae go hame cause it was too early and ma eyes were still like saucers. I just sat drinking and smoking and reading some book I found on the table. From time to time I'd glance over at Laura. She was so stunning. I couldnae believe I'd scuppered ma chance. What if it kept happening? I'd fuckin die a virgin.

I was almost drunk again by the time Thomson appeared.

What's this in here? A fuckin library? he said, wae his heid roon the door.

Couldnae sleep man.

I've no slept either, he said laughing. Your wee bird looks like she's had a good time.

Aye. Are we gaun?

Too right. Gee us ma jaiket, he said.

The road was mobbed. Workies were digging it aw up and the traffic was queued right back. There wur weans on bikes and mothers wae prams and auld guys sauntering aboot. Was worse than the fuckin high street. Everybody seemed tae be staring at us and aw the noise was piercing through ma brain. Felt edgy as fuck.

Hurry up, I said and began tae up the pace.

This is fuckin brutal man, Thomson shouted.

Was like trying tae get aff a battlefield or somethin. I put ma heid doon and tried tae block it aw oot. But I couldnae, I was starting to feel it aw again, this time worse than before. Ma mooth ached and ma heid pounded and there was a hollowness inside I'd never felt before. The paranoia was ramping up and I felt like running.

This way, Thomson said and pulled me intae an alley.

We wur like two guys trying tae get back to basecamp. Heids doon, one foot in front ae the other, trying no tae freak oot, trying no tae collapse. Was the longest walk of ma life and it couldnae've been any further than a half mile. Thomson's maw must've saw us coming cause she was staunin at the front door as we came up the path.

How are yous boys? she said wae a big smile on her face.

Aye, Thomson said. Was some night. Wee Davie Boy took his first eccie and pulled a bird.

Did ye son, she said, as I came in at his back.

Don't think he's feeling too great noo right enough, he added.

Why don't yous go intae the room and lie doon and I'll make yous a coupla rolls.

Aye, that would be nice I said, trying no tae make eye contact.

Any fags Maw? he shouted.

Aye, in the living room.

I laid back on Thomson's bed and tried to think aboot what happened wae Laura. How could the best night ever end like that? It was a fuckin scandal and I only had mysel tae blame. Last night I wis dreaming of a future wae her and noo I was hoping tae never bump intae her again. It was a sore yin awright. I'd the fear aboot anybody finding oot. Especially Thomson, that cunt would tell everybody, and I'd never hear the end ae it. His ears must've been burning cause he appeared wae two cups ae tea and a fag behind each ear.

Gie us that video case up, he said.

This one?

Aye.

I passed it over and he handed me the tea. It was nice

and sugary. He opened the case, took out the weed, and skins, and started building a joint.

Here, he said, passing me a fag and the case. Build yoursel wan.

I canny roll.

For fuck sake Davie Boy. You're gauny need tae learn wan day.

I know, but I don't think today's gaun tae be thiday fur that. I can hardly haud this tea wae oot spilling it.

Take wan ae these, he said and handed me a wee blue pill.

Whit are they?

Valium. Ma maw's. It'll settle ye doon and help ye sleep. Wan a them and a joint and ye'll be sorted.

I'd heard people talking aboot Valium before. I remembered ma maw saying ma grampa wis oan them for his nerves. Mines were fuckin shattered so I didnae think twice aboot taking it. Swallowed it doon wae tea and it left a kinda chalky taste in ma mooth.

Don't say I'm no good tae ye, he said, and handed me a joint.

I felt like I was melting after it, but in a good way. He wis right, I did feel better, and the thoughts aboot last night were starting tae fade. The smell of bacon was wafting in fae the kitchen but the idea of eating anything was beyond me.

Some night though, eh? he said.

Aye, some night awright.

Did ye get that wee bird's number?

Naw. Did you get yours?

Naw. She wisnae as good as I thought she wis.
What aboot yours? he said, just as I was drifting aff.
Whit dae ye mean?
Your bird. How was she?
Awright, aye, I mumbled. Nothing special.

Don't feed the seagulls for they will end up knowing where you live

Kik Lodge

You'll probably pooh-pooh this rule, throw a chip at it, watch a winged creature swallow said chip, creating a sense of connection between you and bird, you and sky, you and Great Beyond.

You'll have no inkling that the bird's entire stepfamily has taken down your address, and come tomorrow, will be outside your beach bolthole with beaks and shopping trolley, banging and tapping until the glass becomes a million replications of itself.

They will puncture beams, just for the hell of it. Prise open the fridge, pull paintings apart.

As you sit in your office-box sending another gull GIF, they will shit on Grandmother's bedspread and back they will be tomorrow with clam puke and copulation calls, forcing you inland (like Mother suggested from the start!) to a nice little cul-de-sac, replicated a million times over, where an easy-to-install security system will send panoramas of said house to your office computer, and would – were an intruder to come too close – unleash a jeremiad of squawks.

Courtauld Institute Galleries

University of London

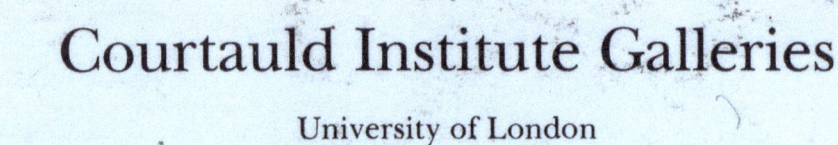

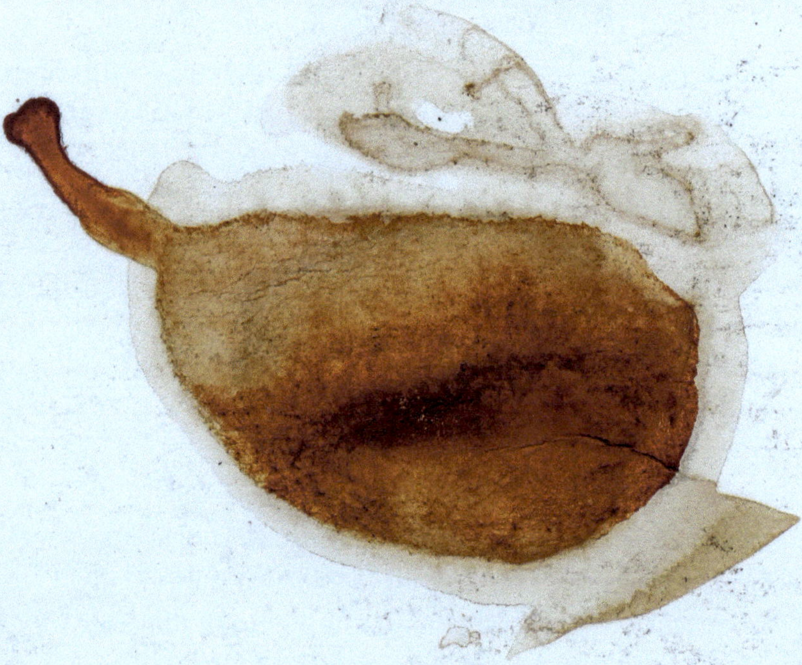

Just another day

Gillian Mayes

We were by the courgettes. I was looking in her trolley: some chocolate biscuits, one candle.

Her shoes were grey – unusual in someone who seems poor. If you're poor, you just have black shoes, or maybe a pair of brown ones too. I hated brown but my mother liked it and I was dressed in brown and green until my teens.

'What's that?' the woman said, pointing.

She had an outdoors sort of face. I don't mean horsey – something she would have been born with. No. This was earned: weather-beaten, moles allowed to grow, more wrinkles than necessary on a woman.

'It's a marrow,' I said.

'And what do you do with it?'

'Soup. I think you can make soup with it. I'm not a great cook.'

'I was, once. In my earlier life.'

Sometimes you linger with people because you think that maybe you're the first person they've talked to all day.

'I was stationed at Bletchley Park in the war,' she went on. 'But I wasn't a cook. They just realised that I was good at it in my digs so I would end up cooking for everyone.'

There had been a programme on television the night before about Bletchley Park.

'Good for you.'

It felt patronising.

'I did far more important work than that.'

'Oh?'

'I'm not allowed to talk about it.'

'Okay. That's great though.'

I moved on to the milk and yoghurt aisle. Five minutes later, we came across each other again. She didn't recognise me. She now had bedding in her trolley. Sheets, downy covers, pillows, it looked like.

'That's a load you've got,' I said.

'My daughter is coming over from Australia next week. I'm refreshing her bedroom. I've had the painter in and. . .'

She gestured to the trolley.

'That's great. You'll be excited to see her.'

'She's not been home for seven years.'

'Goodness. That's a long time. Have you gone out there yourself?'

'I couldn't risk it. You see, because of my work for the government there are certain restrictions on my movements. Let's just say, it wouldn't be wise.'

'Well, have a lovely time when she comes over.'

*

I see her again at the tills, right in front of me. She's speaking to the checkout lady.

'I've got a new lodger coming soon,' she's saying. 'And

there's a baby. I thought I would just buy some things for it. You know, so that the girl could settle in without having to unpack everything.'

Her trolley was filled to the brim with baby things – nappies, formula milk, bottles, dummies, baby toys. . .

'Hello again,' I said to her, as I pushed my trolley forwards and she took her receipt.

She looked at me closely. Said nothing. Then pushed her trolley away towards the door.

Arkansas

Carl Thompson

They met at a party one night in June. He only went because he was helping his cousin, DJ Dave. The house was out of town, on a road all its own. They parked the van round the back and set up in the marquee. He drank Newcastle Brown while Dave drank Red Bull; they watched the guests make their entrances beneath the marquee lights, all the girls technicolour, all the boys black and white. Halfway through the night she came up with her friend and they asked Dave to play Madonna. Her friend did the talking; she hung back with her beer, looked round, caught his eye once or twice. They went back to their dancing and when Dave played 'Borderline' the two girls went wild, jumping around, shouting like crazy. She was drunk and she was cool, way cooler than the rest; she came back a little later, this time alone. She'd got him a beer and she hung around for a while and talked, and she wrote down her number on the palm of his hand.

Dave told him later, You're way out of your depth, mate.

*

Their first date was at a coffee place in town. He was an hour early, and high on caffeine by the time she arrived. He needed a piss but held on as long as he could until it was painful.

When they ran out of things to say she pulled up her sleeve.

Ask me how I got this, she said.

It was a scar that began at her wrist, twisting like rope round the back of her arm. He didn't want to ask.

The fire that killed my little brother, she said. I like to get it out there, so no-one feels bad.

They drank more coffee, then wandered around town in and out of shops with no intention of buying anything. They sat in the square with a pizza. She preferred pigeons to sparrows, which to him made no sense. They talked about exes, and other first dates.

She said, Next time we'll go to the pub.

*

He didn't sleep that night. He stayed up with the radio on, not really listening, waiting for the dawn. His head was always full of nonsense, now it was full of her.

They saw a lot of each other those summer months. She had her own car so they drove everywhere. This car, it was full of stuff, stuff everywhere: piles of clothes and books on the back seat, tins of hairspray and deodorant in the footwell hitting his foot each time they made a turn. Make-up in the ashtray, mixtapes and CDs in the side pockets, shoes and bags in the boot. He once tried to pick up a few things and she slapped him, playfully but hard.

I like my mess, she said. Don't you ever touch it.

The first time they fucked was in that car, amongst the books and piles of clothes.

*

She took him to the pub to meet her friends. He recognised the other girl from the night they first met. She asked how Dave was.

One of the boys said, This the guy you gave a blow job to in the back of his van?

They seemed good company. They laughed a lot and talked a lot. He listened and got drunk and joined in.

They talked about the things they'd done, the places they'd been. He had to ask a lot of questions. He didn't even know the easy stuff. He mispronounced Arkansas. He felt her squeeze his hand as she corrected him.

*

His mother didn't like her. She never said it out loud, but he knew. When he got home from seeing her off at the station, his mother was in the yard. He watched her from the kitchen window as she pegged washing to the line. Next door's cat watched her from the top of the wall.

When she came in she lit a cigarette and sat at the kitchen table. She said, Maybe now she's gone you'll find your head again, son.

*

She wrote to him from university. Her letters were long, and hard to read because she wrote in the margins and upside down and drew pictures and wrote poems and told dirty jokes. She talked about her housemates and her tutors and the films she'd been to see, and how much she missed his face.

He would read these letters over and over again, until he'd taken in all she had to say. Then he would write his reply through the night in a fever, post it on the way to work before he could change his mind, then wait for another purple envelope to drop through the door.

He tried to be honest. Even in those letters, it was never easy. Instead he talked about Dave and the town and the shops closing down and his Friday nights out at the pub.

Her letters always ended by saying he should visit. They talked about it on the phone. She said, You should visit.

I'll hitch.

It'll take forever.

I'll get there when I get there.

A pause.

*

He never visited. Instead he waited for her to come back. While he did he found work at the garage as an apprentice. He'd spend all his wages on a Friday night. He couldn't fight but he tried. He lost his grandfather's watch rolling around on the dance floor in Wunderbar. He turned down a fuck with Jackie Muir. No-one turned down a fuck with Jackie Muir. She took it badly, hit him with a glass ashtray. It didn't break but it left a lump on the back of his head the size of a golf ball.

His mother said, If you carry on like this you'll end up in the jail or the morgue.

*

It got to Easter. It was the year when the snow never stopped. Photographers came from all over to shoot the frozen fountain in the park. His dog Penny broke her leg on the ice and never recovered. She was put down before the thaw.

The snow was her excuse for not coming home.

His apprenticeship came to an end so he spent more time around the house. His mother drove him mad. She had a new boyfriend, Seth. Seth had been a merchant seaman all his life. He had crazy eyes and shit tattoos but he had loads of good stories.

He said things like, The ones that are thick ain't so clever if they think the ones that are clever ain't as thick.

He was full of shite like that. Most nights they sat in the kitchen, shared a half bottle of whisky and a joint while his mother watched TV in bed.

Tell me about this girl, Seth once said.

He thought for a moment.

Nah, he said. Let's talk about something else.

*

He called her in the middle of the night, playing songs down the phone. He played her Elvis Costello and The Beatles and The Clash. She started crying and so did he. She hung up before he got to play 'Borderline'.

the x95

Derek Murray

the bus jolted to a stop and the man
who had been talking to a rucksack
on the seat next to him woke and
shouted for his dead wife. then he
resumed his conversation. the bag
remained inscrutable, not wishing to
commit to a view on the issue being
discussed.
the passengers, scattered around on
other seats, found it more difficult still
than the rucksack to settle on a
position when the driver opened his door,
jumped the fence and ran down a field.
leaving the seated just looking at one
another shaking their heads. perfect i said
to no one. closing my eyes. the answer to
this could never match the question.

Exes

Ian Alexander

The sun had set and it was time for bed. Frank and Pauline switched off the TV: the film had been shite, they could guess the ending. Frank made his way upstairs first. Pauline always poured herself a glass of water before bed, for the peace. She paused with her hands on the edge of the sink and her eyes shut, listening to the creaking and thudding of Frank's footsteps overhead. She took a slow, deep breath and poured the water down the drain.

*

Upstairs, Frank was getting everything ready. He opened up the wardrobe and their exes all came tumbling out. The bodies piled up on top of one another and they fumbled to push off one another and get up. There was Emma and Laura and the one-night stand in Corfu whose name he couldn't remember and that other one he'd rather forget about, Mhairi, so he stuffed her under the bed. Then there were Pauline's: the boyish Jennifer and Chris with his full head of hair.

Frank lined them up so they could get the thing done with

when Pauline was here. He had an early meeting and he wanted to get to bed. He heard Pauline's stupid slow walk up the stairs and in anticipation of the door opening, he refused to look. The door always creaked when it opened. Frank winced.

"Difficult or easy first?" Pauline asked.

"Easy tonight," Frank said.

"Ok. Who you choosing?"

"No, you first."

"You sure?"

"Yes."

*

Pauline took a deep breath, slow and quiet so Frank couldn't hear it. Frank loved to set the agenda, then tell her to go first. Something about chivalry being dead. What was he doing saying easy first?

"Right, how about Jennifer then?"

"Yeah, alright." Frank gestured for Jennifer to get in bed.

Jennifer climbed in, tucking herself straight and flat along the footboard. Pauline imagined running her toes through Jennifer's hair. Christ, her hair had smelt great. Did she still cut it short? She'd rub that oil in after getting out the shower. Pauline used to seek it out in the shops, long after they broke up. They didn't make it anymore.

But Frank had never taken Jennifer seriously: bisexuality didn't exist. Deep down, he probably thought he had a magic penis that turned her straight.

*

Frank didn't get the Jennifer thing. It had been a phase and in all honesty – though he'd never say it – Jennifer wasn't really that good-looking. Surely if you are into women you are into women. But Jennifer was so androgynous with the short hair and sharp jawline. Laughing when Pauline said she'd proposed had been the wrong thing but come on. The fact the one woman she'd been with had looked like a schoolboy was just more evidence she had never been a lesbian.

"Your turn," said Pauline.

Of course it was his turn. He wasn't an idiot. He'd take his sweet fucking time if he wanted. He milked it even though he knew Emma was easiest to place next. Tapped his toes a bit. Shifted his weight and scratched his cheek. His phone buzzed on the bedside table but he ignored it. Probably Mhairi.

"Emma can go in next," Frank declared.

"Whereabouts though?"

Frank thought a minute. Honestly he didn't care. His time with Emma was a vague fog at the bottom of a valley he never ventured into. He'd met Emma in uni and it had been his first success, but looking back he didn't understand what had happened. It just was. Like two soggy cardboard puzzle pieces that sort of fit together.

He couldn't even remember what they talked about. They'd have sex because it's what you did but he didn't think they'd ever fucked. And somewhere along the line he'd proposed. It's what you did after all. But they'd mistaken the absence of conflict as love until the greater terror of forever had reached them both. And at some point before the wedding Frank came home to a letter on the table and surprised himself as he cried – not from despair but relief.

Now the only problem that remained was where to put her pale body each night. He could stick her at the foot with Jennifer but it was hard to get to sleep unless he could stretch out. She wasn't important enough to go between him and Pauline. But Pauline had always balked at the fact he felt that way about a former fiancée.

"Pillow," Frank decided.

Pauline made that face that let Frank know she thought he was wrong.

*

Emma clambered on to the bed and curled up into a ball on Frank's side.

"My turn?" Pauline asked.

"Yeah, obviously."

Yeah obviously, but Frank would be even more pissy if Pauline just went without asking. And Emma as the pillow? She had so much hair. Frank would be tossing, and turning, and spitting it out of his mouth all night. Pauline had suggested a hairnet, but obviously it was a shite idea because it had come from Pauline.

Frank's phone buzzed again and Pauline watched him dismiss the notifications.

"Ok, I'll take Laura," said Pauline.

"Laura?"

"Yes, Laura."

Frank's jaw clenched. "She's not one of yours though," he balked. "You've only got the one woman."

"Yeah, but we've been over this: you have more exes than I do," Christ knows he loved the fact, "and you don't like going twice in a row at the end."

Pauline watched the gears turn in Frank's gormless head. "It's not exactly my fault I've had more success than you."

"Ok, well for tonight I'll help by picking where Laura goes."

Frank conceded with a burrowing silence.

Pauline had known Laura. Not well, but enough for Pauline to know she didn't care for her. It was when Pauline still went out with some of the girls that she hadn't lost touch with since Jen. Laura was one of their flatmates or something, and she had brought her newish man. Pauline was a bit high, a bit drunk, and a bit bored, and Frank was entertaining. When they'd kissed under the patio heater outside, Laura had seen them and thrown her drink. Sticky with rum and mixer, Pauline and Frank had scurried laughing into the night.

"She can go on my side," said Pauline.

*

Laura slinked flat-chested and pathetic into the far side of the bed.

This was too fucking much. Her side? He wasn't going to rise to it. But he knew how to get back at her.

"Ok," said Frank, "I pick Corfu. Your pillow."

He knew that would wind Pauline up.

Corfu was his stag do. It was too late to cancel the flights and hotels even though Emma had gone. But it had been a great week. Fantastic beaches and plenty of drink to fill the hollow. And then on the last evening before their flight home him and his pals were at a bar and none of them could take their eyes off her – Ms Corfu.

So they invited her over to join them. They'd fought amongst themselves for her attention. Ever louder and lewder. Competing for a bit of laughter. Then as the night went on she'd learnt why they were in her sunny little corner of the world and the pity had given way to intimacy at least for a night.

Frank struggled to remember what she really looked like except from the eyebrows and the lips – both full and strong in a way that wasn't in style back home. But he'd felt a new road paved before him on returning home and knew that he need not fear. If not worthy of women's love then at least of their bodies. And maybe that was better.

But the months had become a year or more and Frank felt the assurance fading. He could make them laugh – oh how he could make them laugh – but never more. Until Laura. She laughed too hard and, swayed with drink, invited him back to hers. And Frank saw a chance to believe in himself again.

Then a few months later he was getting introduced to Laura's friends and he'd made some remark in Pauline's direction and she'd said something he didn't have a comeback to. He couldn't remember what. Just that it had put him in his place. So he followed her out for a smoke. And he didn't really care for Laura beyond convenience and this girl before him was even funnier on her own so he leant in and got lost in her. Then after some time he heard a scream and felt a plastic cup hit his head and liquid run down his back. He turned round ready to beg forgiveness but this new girl laughed. Laughed! So he laughed too as they fucked off back to his. And maybe he still had it.

*

Pauline couldn't believe Frank was making Corfu into her pillow. Again. His favourite revenge move when it wasn't going his way. She'd never tell him, but she was convinced Corfu had been an escort his pals had hired. It was in the little jokes that only came when Frank was in the bathroom or out for a smoke.

But Frank's skull was filled with a thick, glaekit sludge and he had missed what Pauline's only remaining choice was. So it was time to act defeated. To protest, and kowtow, and concede defeat in a game with no winners.

"That's ridiculous. She doesn't need to be my pillow. I never think about her." Which was true, but she knew Frank believed it a lie.

"I don't see where else she can go," Frank said, failing to contain his self-satisfied smirk. "I know you hate it when she's beside me."

Pauline crossed her arms and furrowed her brow. She didn't hate it. All she'd done was ask him to stop wanking a few times because she wanted to get to sleep.

"Fine." Pauline threw up her arms to really sell it.

Pauline watched Frank grin as Corfu clambered over

Laura and curled up alongside Frank's ex-fiancée, who, honestly, you would hope he cared more about than a one-night stand.

It was all a bit sad. Frank didn't even know her name and couldn't really remember what she looked like. Here on their bed, forged from Frank's memories of the encounter, she was reduced to an indistinct face with big lips and a set of almost comical tits. Then there was the fact he considered a one-night stand to be an ex. Pauline imagined if she did the same: the pile of bodies they'd have to sleep on. How it would shatter the illusion Frank had built for himself. Nothing seemed to matter more to him than his unfulfilled potential as sexual conquistador. That's what he wanked to. Not the encounter with Corfu herself, but the deluded promise that out there waiting were as many such nights as he desired.

But Frank had wasted his turn. And now it was Pauline's.

"Well, all that's left is Chris." Pauline relished in watching Frank's face drop. "So I suppose he has to go on your side."

Frank's mouth chewed on his panic. His phone went off again and he shoved it in the bedside drawer.

"No, he shouldn't go on my side," Frank said.

"Well, where else can he go?" Pauline feigned concern.

"Between us," said Frank.

"Between us?" Pauline knew Frank never wanted Chris to be anywhere near him, but also nowhere near Pauline. Only the foot of the bed, and so Pauline never put him there. After all, what if she thought about her past lover? That wouldn't do.

So Pauline watched the cogs spin and the confused babbling as he changed his mind each time, his mouth flapping like a fish pulled from water. Yes, no, yes, no, yes, no. But eventually, as she predicted:

"No."

Pauline watched Frank stare as Chris lay down on Frank's side of the bed. Pauline imagined Frank was wondering who had a larger penis again.

Chris had been Pauline's first boyfriend. He was tall, and blonde, and fit, played rugby, and had good marks, and all the girls fancied him, but he had chosen her. Her. That had meant everything to the insecure teenager she had been. But it was that desperation to please that had got her chosen. So she'd known he was talking to other girls, but she didn't dare to ask about them. Then it was their third year at uni, and she hadn't seen him in person for weeks, so she went round to his flat despite knowing what she would find.

Now, Pauline hadn't cared for years. Chris had been a prick and it didn't reflect on her. So Pauline clambered over Laura, and lay her head on Corfu, and ran her toes through Jennifer's hair, because it was finally time for bed.

*

Frank couldn't believe Pauline could just climb into bed like that. Pretending. Frank was determined to appear to not care himself. Without touching Chris. But as he climbed on top of the bedside table Mhairi grabbed at his ankle from under the bed. Frank tumbled face first into Chris's back.

Pauline guffawed. Frank took out his frustration on Mhairi's hand and kicked it back under the bed.

"What are you kicking?" asked Pauline.

Shit. "Nothing."

"Nothing?"

"Yes."

"If it's nothing, then why are you kicking it?"

What could be under the bed that he wouldn't want her to see? But also she wouldn't want to look at?

"It's your birthday present."

"No it's not, Frank."

"Yes it is."

"No, my birthday was two months ago and you forgot about it."

"Yeah, well." Fuck. "That's why I've planned so far in advance. To make it up to you."

Pauline pulled back the duvet and tapped Laura on the shoulder, telling that ex of Frank's to sit up. Pauline swung round and out of bed to see what Frank was hiding underneath.

"Who the fuck is this, Frank?"

"Nobody."

"Is it nobody? Or is it my birthday present?"

Frank was fucked. "Both?"

*

"I suppose this is who's been texting you then?"

Pauline wasn't even sad or angry. An aching lightness, like removing a backpack you've worn so long you forgot it was ever heavy.

"Come on Pauline."

Pauline wasn't sure where she was going, but that could be figured out on the road. She fetched a rucksack from the wardrobe. It could fit a week's worth of clothes and some essentials easy.

"For fuck's sake Pauline."

Pauline packed what clothes she'd need for the office first. The boring blouses and cardigans that offended nobody and could be endlessly combined with one another.

"There's no need to be so childish about this Pauline."

She was going to need to go out at the weekend. She hadn't had fun in a while. So much catching up to do with people she hadn't seen in months. Pish movie after pish TV show and the weekends had dissolved into the weeks. Christ, she hadn't had fun in a while.

"Just hear me out."

What was she going to wear when she came to pick stuff up? Maybe that one dress Frank liked because she had worn it the first time they hooked up? No, that'd seem desperate, like she wanted to get back together. Maybe that one outfit he hated because he thought it was too goth? Still dressy maybe. Maybe she'd send someone else round and save herself the headache.

"It was just – it wasn't even fun. It's over now."

Toothbrush, toothpaste. It was obviously over, or she wouldn't be under the bed. Frank hovered by the bathroom, and in her periphery Pauline saw his hands wring.

"Just listen to me Pauline."

But she had been halfway out the door, and this was the

perfect excuse. She considered thanking him, but would never. Obviously. Where was her handbag?

"I'll do whatever it takes. Just tell me how to fix it."

He probably just hated that it wasn't him who had chosen to leave. Pauline fished for her keys so she could leave them behind. She opened the door but something was missing.

"Pauline. Come on."

Ah, her other exes.

*

"Pauline, don't do this to me. Come on."

Frank felt it again. Like thrashing in the open ocean. Pauline was heading back up the stairs.

"Please, Pauline. It was a one-time thing."

And it had been. A stupid one-time thing after going out for drinks at work and only him and the doe-eyed intern were still standing. Then the fear had crept into Frank. What if he couldn't get with anyone better than Pauline? What if this was his last chance? But it turned out that Mhairi's laugh was annoying and she wasn't any good in bed and she was so keen to please that it didn't feel like an achievement at all. So now he had to hide in the stationery cupboard and ignore texts.

Pauline stepped out and shut the door behind her and Frank watched himself from the window as he joined Chris and Jennifer and the three of them together followed Pauline away down the road.

Concrete

Mel Piper

Her skin is cracking.

She is trying to shave, standing in the bathroom, her leg up on the side of the tub. She takes away the stubble, hopes she won't cut herself too many times. But, instead of blood, she sees light. She thinks she is dreaming at first, but it's there. There are patches of light on her arms, and her chest. There is one on her pinkie toe. The light is warm, and when she goes to touch it, it feels soft.

She hasn't had this sensation for a while. And definitely not to this extent. She likes her concrete armour. It stops her from getting hurt. But the light is comforting. Scary, but comforting. The idea that one day, her concrete skin will be replaced by light fills her with pleasure.

Carrying on, she is careful not to shave the cracks. Satisfied, she takes out lotion, and rubs it all over. The skin is softening in other places too. There's now a crack growing from the corner of her lips. She opens and closes her mouth, but it doesn't hurt. If anything, she wants to lay herself open, talk about her fears, her deepest secrets, the madness that she doesn't let anyone else see.

Her partner is next door. They're fast asleep, could sleep through anything.

She wonders if their skin is cracking too.

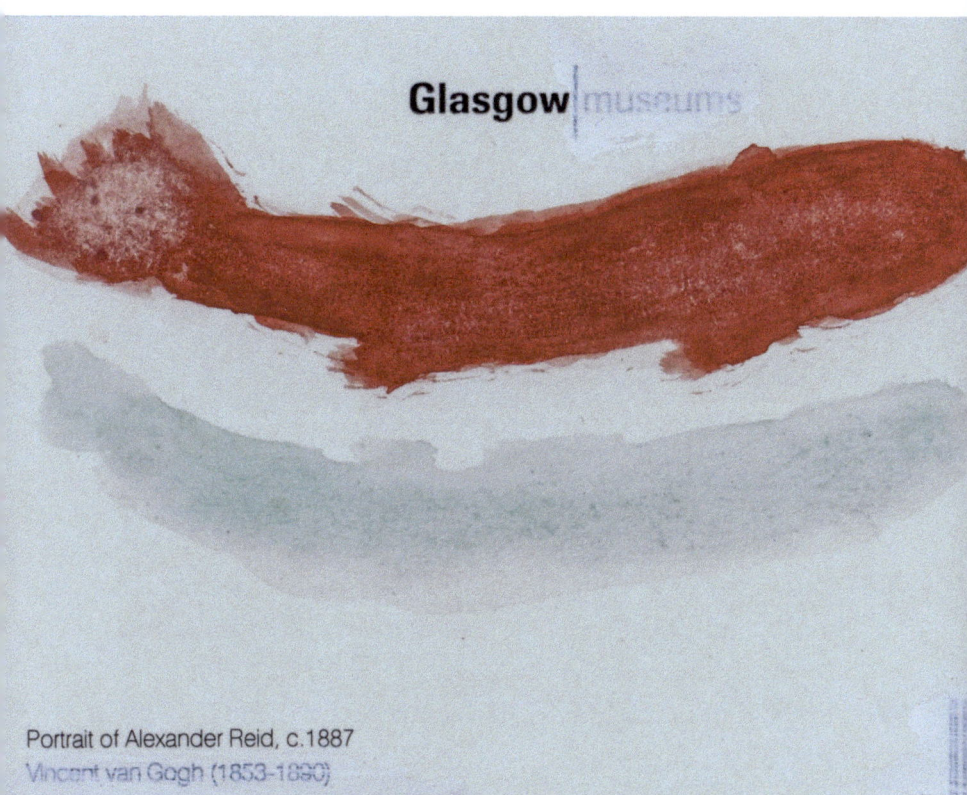

Glasgow museums

Portrait of Alexander Reid, c.1887
Vincent van Gogh (1853-1890)
© CSG CIC Glasgow Museums Collection

Working from Home

Simran Kaur

I sit in front of my laptop with my webcam on, waiting for my manager to join the Zoom call. My childhood desk in my childhood bedroom, the cheap wood damaged and worn from years of use. I'm nervous. *It'll be over soon.* Then I can get back to work.

The camera me is a grainy, pixelated mirror that makes the shadows on my face look like thick black paint, oozing. The lighting has never been good in this spot, worsened by the winter sky sucking out the saturation. I move my jaw backwards and forwards to see which position minimises the appearance of a double chin. I tuck it in and poke it out again. Unflattering. Maybe I should buy a ring light. Or a fancier webcam. Is that vain?

I can't imagine it's particularly healthy to stare at yourself like this for prolonged periods of time. I open up the text I'm translating for one of our main clients and find the sentence I left off from, but I can't push the words past my eyes and into my brain.

All'aeroporto, si sono ridotte anche le emissioni indirette grazie al coinvolgimento degli stakeholder.

At the airport, we have reduced...No.
*At the airport, indirect emissions have been reduced...*reduced or decreased? Which is better?

I'm not making any progress. This isn't a good use of my time. I flick between the Word document and Zoom, just to keep my hands occupied.

Above my head, Zoom informs me that the meeting room has now been open for 24 minutes and 12 seconds. That's how long the camera has been on me. The version of me on screen has evolved into a weird twin I didn't know existed. You'd only notice the differences if you looked really hard. This is the version of me that my manager would see, something not quite right, something that could resemble a normal person if she made more effort. I open Amazon, search for a ring light, and put an averagely-priced one in my basket.

She's late. Really late. I wouldn't have dared to be even a minute late. For the last few days, my anxiety over this meeting has been stewing, growing mould. I will these moments to pass quicker, to force the lump in my throat down. I wipe my sweaty hands on my leggings.

The probation meeting was to cover three main areas of my performance: word count, quality, and speed. Essentially, could I churn out as many words as possible with as few client complaints as possible? Did I produce more in profits than what I cost the company? Would I get in trouble for googling Jobseeker's Allowance on my company-issued laptop?

This whole thing could probably have been done by email. *Hi Harpreet, you can turn off your Indeed notifications.*

God, this waiting! Maybe I can trick myself into forgetting about the passage of time. I grab my phone and open up Twitter. An article about the most recent government scandal. Some hot take I can't fully appreciate. An ad encouraging me to join the army. A poorly thought-out meme with an outdated format. An article about a fish found with over 35 microplastics in its body. That can't be good. I open it and read the first two sentences before being blocked by the paywall.

As the minutes pass, I feel tears prickle behind my eyes. Disappointment. I close Zoom and write my manager an email to reschedule.

Subject: Probation Meeting

Hi Stephanie,

I hope this email finds you well! I'm just writing to see if we can reschedule my probation meeting. Let me know what time works for you! :)

Best wishes,
Harpreet

My throat feels tight and swollen. Just for a moment I allow the frustration to surge, and then fizzle out into silent tears.

Well, if Stephanie has better things to do than show up

to our meeting, then firing me clearly isn't a priority. I force long, deep breaths to steady myself. *Don't cry. Don't cry.* I squeeze my fists and concentrate on the feeling of the muscles in my fingers contracting, the heat of my breath as it leaves my mouth, the pressure of my eyelids on my eyeballs as they close. *Don't cry. Don't cry. You need to get back to work.* After a few moments, the intensity of emotion leaves my body, my jaw unclenches and my shoulders fall. *I still have a job. I didn't get fired today. It's okay. Just focus on today.*

I take off my glasses and roughly wipe off the tears with the sleeve of my jumper, blow my nose, and go back to my text, which is due the next day. I've lost an hour, and with only two hours left in the working day, I still have over 2,000 words to complete. *Focus.*

In order to make the translation as uncomplicated and as easy as possible, I decode the words as though they are binary units of information: little sealed boxes with their meaning contained inside them, untouched by context, the human condition, or the complexity of the world.

All'aeroporto, si sono ridotte anche le emissioni indirette grazie al coinvolgimento degli stakeholder. Gli investimenti incoraggiano approcci innovativi in grado di promuovere elevati livelli di riciclaggio. . .

At the airport indirect emissions also decreased thanks to the involvement of stakeholders. Investments encourage new. . .no. . .innovative approaches that can promote elevated levels. . .that doesn't sound right in English. . .of recycling. . .

It's wrong and unintuitive, denying the words any fluidity or agency, alienating them from one another, but it's the most efficient way. Language shouldn't be caged like that, but there's no time for any of those luxuries when you have thousands of words to produce a day. It could have been done by a machine. And probably soon, it will be. I chip away at the word count, like placing individual grains of rice into a bowl. Daylight is fading.

I'm pulled out by the Messenger notification. It's Amy.
How did it go? Are you still with us?
I pause. *For now, I guess. Stephanie didn't show up :(*
What! Ugh, I'm sorry. But no news is good news! Drinks later?

*

Every so often, I glance at Microsoft Teams or my emails to see if Stephanie has tried to get in contact, but there is nothing. Her Teams icon indicates that she has been online.

I don't finish the translation until half an hour after my shift ends. I give it a half-hearted once-over before sending it to the project manager. Objectively, it is a bad piece of work. I am not proud of it.

Opening my phone again, I am reminded of the fish that was found stuffed with microplastics and I feel deeply sad for it. I wonder if there are any microplastics inside me right now.

A Nice Guy

Wayne Dean-Richards

I felt like shit warmed up. Three nights on the piss was why. Discovered if you drank enough of it your sweat stank like Breaker.

"What the fuck are you playing at, Ronnie?" Alison had snapped. In the middle of the night this was. I'd been palming Breaker-stinking sweat from my face and slipped – fallen backwards downstairs and puked. If the noise hadn't woken her, I might have drowned in my own fucking vomit. Couldn't answer her question then because I didn't know what the fuck I was playing at, and still couldn't answer it when it came back at me as I was steering a shopping trolley towards the booze aisle.

Never mind, I told myself. Told myself everything would be alright so long as I didn't buy Breaker. Was telling myself Carling or Bud would be OK. I liked Carling better than Bud, but Carling reminded me of my old man and thinking about my old man distracted me. That was when our trollies collided.

It was me who wasn't looking where I was going but he was the one who said, "Sorry," and smiled.

His smile spelled out in no uncertain terms that he hadn't ever drunk Breaker till his sweat stank of it, and wasn't somebody whose wife had found him covered in vomit and asked him what the fuck he was playing at, so I stomped off.

But when my Carling was being scanned, I saw him again: at the checkout next to me, so close I heard his checkout wasn't just chatting to be polite. A proper conversation was what they were having and once it was finished, I watched him leave the supermarket ahead of me, steering his trolley in a straight line.

I hurried after him.

Outside the supermarket, the front wheel of my shopping trolley caught the edge of one of the speed bumps and I fell to my knees. Carling, beans, and bread spilled out. Was still that way when the nice guy rushed over. Righted my shopping trolley then scooped up the bread, the beans, my Carling. Smiled and said, "There you are." Was reaching out to help me up when I hit him.

Sharp as a new razor Alison's question came back at me.

I screamed by way of answer. Wiped tears from my eyes as my throat closed off and people ran towards us.

fifty first states (Extract)

Joanne Thomson

Jess was a host of people, of travellers, boys and pain. In that order. People would come to her. Give me a home, they'd say. Give me a home for a night or two or a year. Sometimes they'd pay, sometimes they wouldn't. Now she wished more had paid. But in the summer of 2014, only guests paid. The boys she took in for free, and only if she thought they really loved her. . .or could. She hadn't allowed herself to have one-offs. What was the point? She hated sex. When she was little her Mum had told her sex was a special gift from God. At fifteen she thought she'd test that theory with her boyfriend Mark on a bunk bed at her friend Tam's house. It was the worst pain she'd ever felt and she bled on his stale bedsheets. Afterwards, while they were still lying next to each other, Mark said if she got pregnant he'd rip it out with a coat hanger and throw it in front of a lorry. He laughed. So did she. Thanks for giving me the *gift* of Mark, God. He's so funny.

    Somewhere inside this need to host foreign bodies she'd seen an opportunity: Airbnb. Her Mum stayed in one when she'd gone to Berlin as part of an end-of-life crisis. She'd wanted to practise her German and the thick Glaswegian accent often fooled people into thinking she was legit, until they'd answer her back in German and she'd have to break character to apologise. But still, she found contentment sitting in her mobility scooter at Checkpoint Charlie with two wheels on the right of where the wall had been and two wheels on the left: a divided concept Jess had never quite grasped.

Back then the phrase BnB sounded weird with Air in front of it. Now it seemed alien without it. *That's* branding. During her summer breaks from university, Jess had popped her place on there. How novel. Strangers in your house. You could make money while you slept and all you had to do in return was hope they didn't creep in your room and kill you. Jess was pretty certain they wouldn't. The company took their card details so it would be a pretty shit crime. There was a part of her that liked the risk and either way, it meant she wasn't lonely. She hated being alone. She took in all sorts. Her place was small, and it only had one bathroom and the water pressure was awful. But still, she'd bounce around and grin from ear to ear when she welcomed them with a Tunnock's teacake and a map of Glasgow on their towels. It had all the local spots that locals said to visit. This was to avoid them asking her, a local, where they should go. . .because she didn't know. She'd lived there for over two decades and everything had drifted right past her. Her fingers would trace these fold-up maps (she'd got hundreds for free from a local library) and at every landmark she'd retrace her steps. . .places she'd been – places she hadn't. Most of them had some sort of tainted memory. This city was not her own. She was a tourist, just like them.

A boy she was seeing at the time lived only one street up from her. She didn't realise that when they'd started speaking but it came in very handy. She'd often walk up the hill to his place in her pajamas. Why bother dressing? It also meant that when she opened her door to strangers she had somewhere else to go. Let them get settled in. Once she left having checked in an elderly couple but realising she'd forgotten her phone, returned to find the old woman rummaging through the drawers in Jess's room. Her underwear drawers.

Ummmm. . .

Jesus – you gave me a fright.

Yeh. . .are you ok?

You've not given us any towels.

Yes I did.

No you've not.

They're–

Go on – show us them then. You've not given us any towels.

Jess slid in through the guest room door, the woman's husband clearly mortified at his wife (Miriam Margolyes without the lovability).

Ethel, it's fine. We can–

No, George I'm telling her. She's not given us any–

They're there, Jess said.

Where?

There. Under your coats.

. . .oh.

This was also the couple that told her they'd broken her shower. Jess got an emergency plumber out only for him to discover they just hadn't turned it on. She swore then she wouldn't take any guests over fifty. Which was horribly ageist but over fifty you just had certain expectations of life, and those in it. She had secondhand IKEA furniture and a couple of spare teabags if you needed them. Over fifties wanted the Waldorf Astoria and were bitter that they couldn't afford it. But then she'd never say no. Not really. She'd say *thanks so much for your message – I actually have a friend staying that weekend and she only told me about it yesterday, so I haven't had a chance to update the calendar. . .*y'know – if she didn't like the look of someone. But on the whole, she was pretty lax with the whole thing. She'd got so lax that she started advertising on another website altogether: HomeStay4U. God knows what checks they did. They used 2004 txt abbreviations so probably none. At this point it seemed like a dare to see how long it would take until she got robbed or murdered. But it was a game, the same little game she'd play with herself when she'd see how many days she could go without drinking water. Past day four felt like she was defying the laws of biology. Thrilling. *I'm still alive motherfuckers. My face looks like a testicle but I'm still here.* Nothing makes you feel more alive than defying death every day.

On HomeStay4U they didn't run on reviews. They ran on pure trust. On a Tuesday afternoon Jess got a call from a very disgruntled guest who was due to check in the next day. Nicole. Jess had been in touch with her via email to let her know the arrangements for checking in and Nicole was very surprised to hear that Jess in fact lived in the property too.

Yeh – sorry, it – it says it on the first line of the description. It's a two-bedroom flat and I live in the other room.

Right. But–

I'm sorry.

Do you have a separate entrance to the property?

No, sorry it's a flat. There's just the one door in.

Right. It's just – for the men. . .

. . .the men.

Yeh. I'm a. . .I'm a working woman.

. . .okay?

I work. For money.

Me too.

No. I am a *working* woman.

Ah. Right.

I'm on tour.

Is that – ok. . .

I have men booked in for the full five days. This is unacceptable. I thought I'd have the place to myself.

Um. . .sorry, just so we're on the same page, you were planning on running an illegal business from my flat while I wasn't there?

It is legal. But obviously – right. So how do I cancel?

Click the button on the top right.

What button?

Nicole couldn't find the button so Jess logged into her account for her and found a slew of bookings up and down the country. Nicole was a busy woman. Jess thought of Nicole often, the more she learned about love. About the *cost* of loving, and living. She remembered how affronted she'd been on that call. How she laughed with her friends about it the next day. She'd posted it on Facebook and everyone had laughed at Nicole there too. Maybe they hadn't been laughing at her. Maybe they'd been laughing at Jess. Silly Jess. Didn't she know she was missing a trick? Everyone was paying for sex in some way or another. The only difference was this pay could be exchanged for food. Clothes. The gas bill that kept you warm in a way no person could. Sometimes she stared at the radiator on her wall when she found herself in that familiar state of procrastination. It was one of those storage heaters that saved up their heat during the night when the rates were cheaper. And they slowly let out their gifts through the sunshine hours. They're so clever. What a clever system. But what makes the night cheaper, she wondered? She came alive at night. Always at 2am, after the heaters had expelled all they had left. Now was the banking time. Banking up all that heat for another day. She's paying that radiator for heat. Why shouldn't someone pay Nicole for heat too? Wherever she was, Jess wished her well. She's clued in on something the rest of us were way too slow to figure out. Fair play, Nicole. Fair play tae ye.

Three ways to travel

John G. Hall

an orange, half an orange, a spiral of peel,
fingers, fingers and mouth, bite marks,

wide eyed, moist corners, sly looks,
warm hands, spinal spoons, a cold back,

eyes on eyes, us in a river of sweat, us
in the dry lines of the divorce papers nisi,

a rising breath, a head asleep on a heart's
drum beat, a sigh inside a phone's earpiece.

The Exorcism of PTSD

John G. Hall

I try to be haunted
by the good ghosts
the tiny hand holding
Llandudno jellyfish or
the eight hour football
match or launching

helicopter sycamore or meeting
Alice in Wonderland and the white
rabbit stoned on the West shore or
the man at the far post or the sound
of thousands of tongues singing or

each alien child's paradisal Christmas
eyes wide as dinner plates and the blessed
Johnny 7 aimed at the eagle-eyed action man
dressed as a spaceman next to my Apollo 11

or the long walk home in the rain in love
or the perfect pass right across field to
white who crossed it onto my deadly toe

or the central library of books where
on wet days I first met William Blake and
began to reel in his ball of gold

be haunted by the good ghosts
let the nightmares become alone
why choose only darkest blue from
your jumbo soul's rainbow contrail
be haunted by the good ghosts

they need you to need them
live again to rattle in your sweet
microtubules ringing in your brain
love's forest fire out of control

be haunted by the good ghosts
let them be what you carry home.

The Baths

Pamela McLean

The swimming baths had gone mouldy – yellow spores and green scum and black water. There was a toilet stink everywhere and all kinds of crap underfoot. Broken glass. Fag ends. Mud and feathers. Every step he took felt gritty. Danny imagined swimming in it and almost boaked. You'd be mad to go in it. Imagine the diseases you'd get.

Some of the rooflights were open, and he wondered if anyone else was up there. He thought he could see a shadow. Him and Michael could have come in through the roof, but the rusty padlock was broken and it had been easy to shove their way in through the door. Was it breaking and entering if you didn't have to break anything to get in?

He watched Michael kick a rusty can into the deep end. He'd have been a great striker if he had less chub and spent less time in Drama. Or bothered to turn up for any of the trials.

'Remember the guy that taught us the backstroke? Him with the fucking ponytail? He was a pure pervert so he was.'

It took Danny a second to work out who Michael meant. 'Scott? No man, he was alright.'

'Pervert.'

Danny didn't argue. Best not to with Michael, it could go anywhere. They could end up fighting. Then one of them could end up in the pool and die of some watery disease. He couldn't die on the last day of school. Not when he had uni to look forward to and a whole summer with Laura.

'We getting started then?' Michael nodded at the carry-out Danny was holding.

'We could crack one open when we get to Robbo's.'

But Michael shook his head. 'No time like the present time, Danny Boy. Toss us a can.' He sang the last part and the notes rose to the roof.

Did he mean throw it over the water? Danny reached into the bag for a Tennent's but he took his time. He couldn't throw it, it might not clear the length. All those dense golden bubbles sinking to the bottom of all that murk.

'D'you mind that brick they used to throw in the water?' Danny said.

'What do you mean?'

'The rubber brick that was really heavy so it would sink to the bottom? You'd have to dive to get it.'

Michael was smiling. It always made his face look rounder. 'Rubber prick, I thought you said.'

'D'you not remember it then.'

'I was first to dive down and get it, course I remember. You gonna toss it or not?'

Danny threw the can and Michael caught it. He grinned. 'Tosser.'

Michael cracked open the Tennent's, drank and burped.

Danny was surprised it didn't echo round the baths. Their voices didn't seem to carry the way they had during their lessons. Maybe the mould absorbed the sound, or it was escaping through the rooflights.

'Should we not head round to Robbo's now?' Danny knew he'd made a mistake as soon as he said it.

'Shall we head to the ball, good sir?' Michael crowed. He was enjoying himself. 'Mayhap we should have RSVP'd in advance, but no matter. To the festivities ahead!'

Mr Gordon was going to lose it when he found out Michael wasn't going to RSAMD. 'Arse-mad', Michael called it. He'd been in all the school shows since first year. He could do any accent and change the way he moved and – honest to God – you weren't watching Michael anymore but getting a glimpse of someone else instead. He could act but he'd bombed the audition, maybe to impress Robbo or some of the others, Danny wasn't sure. His mum had signed him up for an apprenticeship instead and Michael said he wasn't bothered. 'It's for homos, Danny. Better off out of it.'

Fair enough – it was his life – but he'd lied to Gordo and made him believe he was heading off to drama school. A success story for the department. Suppose that showed you he really could act but Robbo had clapped Michael on the back as if he'd got one over on everyone. Danny had never seen anyone congratulate Michael before. Just six years of slagging for being in all the school plays.

'What are we doing here, man?'

'One last hurrah. I told you Danny, they're going to tear it down one day and build posh flats because it's in an up-and-coming area.' He had the BBC accent down to a tee.

'How'd you even know that?'

'I follow the local news. Unlike some.' Michael raised an eyebrow. 'Why aren't you drinking?'

'I'm not wasting good beer on this, I'm saving it for Robbo's.'

'Saving it for the lovely Laura you mean.'

'Give it a rest.'

'Tonight's the night!' Michael's sudden burst of song caused a ripple of wing flapping near the roof. Pigeon nest. 'It's gonna be alright!'

'Fucksake Michael, don't bring Rod Stewart into this.'

'Think you'll need to bring in old Hot Rod for Laura.'

And Danny knew why they'd come. He looked over at the changing cubicles, the sky-blue paint all dotted with decay. The baths had always been so warm. A dry heat when you slipped out of your school clothes and then a heavy heat afterwards when you rolled off your trunks and wrapped yourself in a scratchy towel. Him and Michael got the same cubicle every week, made it there before the other kids from their class did and were first out the water at the end of lessons. It was the best cubicle, the one at the end, furthest from the front door and right next to the heavy ridged radiator with the peeling white flakes – the warmest place in the whole baths.

They used to take ages changing. Michael would overbalance trying to put on his socks and trainers and Danny spent forever towel drying so his clothes wouldn't stick to him. They did it every Friday until the week Danny looked down and saw that Michael had hair on his balls. It wasn't a lot but it was shocking. He couldn't stop sneaking looks. Danny had nothing down there, no hair or anything, but Michael looked like a man and he felt like a child. He was ashamed even before Michael caught him looking, and it was one of those moments when you're properly caught, no way out of it. Danny knelt and fumbled to put his trainers on. He could feel the blush start its creep up his skin and he was trying to leave before Michael saw that too but when he turned around, head down to mumble 'bye', he saw that Michael had a semi. Danny turned and pushed open the swing doors to get out, trainers squeaking and almost slipping on the tiles as he headed towards the front door.

Danny hadn't thought of it in years. He'd spent that whole weekend dreading seeing Michael on the Monday, but Michael acted like nothing happened. It never got mentioned. When Danny got a different cubicle the next week that never got mentioned either. They stopped swimming when they went to secondary anyway, and the baths had been closed for the last few years. There had been no reason to think about it.

Michael saw him looking towards the cubicles.

'Best one, remember? D'you mind playing at cowboys?'

That was right, that's how Danny had been able to burst out of the cubicle so quickly. The doors didn't lock and they met in the middle, swinging in and out like saloon doors. Michael had been good at the cowboy accent, he'd watched a lot of westerns with his dad. They'd got in trouble more than once for launching out of the changing rooms and shouting at whoever was passing. It had been a good laugh.

'Aye,' said Danny. 'You were always watching westerns.'

Danny used to watch them too. Michael's dad would nod at him from his armchair, and he and Michael would sit on the sofa with a can of Tango each, a multipack of pickled-onion Space Raiders between them. His dad would leave the room every so often to get a beer or go to the toilet, and Danny would look at the depressed grooves he left on his armchair. It must have took a lot of sitting to get it that way. Danny's mother would have had a fit.

There'd been a lot of Saturdays like that. They had been working their way through John Wayne's films and one week Michael told him that John Wayne's real name was Marion. Danny wouldn't believe him until his dad confirmed it. Marion Robert Morrison. Why did he have a lassie's name? He felt let down. He wondered if Michael had too.

'D'you mind the time you told me John Wayne's real name?'

Michael smiled but froze when he heard a crack from above. They both looked up and saw shadows flanking the rooflights; the outlines of two people lying on the glass, silhouetted against the sun. There was a long crack underneath one of them and as they watched, it spread and spiderwebbed across the glass. Danny held his breath and then everything happened at once: the glass fractured and dropped, a boy starfished through the air and bellyflopped into the pool. Murky water crested and slopped over the edges. Danny got splashed but Michael was drenched. He still had the can of Tennent's in his hand.

There was no movement in the pool except for the slosh of water and glints of glass on the surface.

'Fucksake man, help him!' The voice from the roof was frantic. 'Get him out!'

Michael was nearer. He looked at Danny a long moment and seemed to realise he wasn't going to make a move. Danny could see the moment Michael decided to cannonball in. He didn't look over again, just held his breath and jumped in. Danny watched him pinball back and forth to the surface, up and down, back and forth, for a minute, maybe more, until Danny felt like he was going to be sick.

'Move it, get him out!' The voice from the roof again. Another boy. Danny stumbled to the deep end and felt his trainers slip on a slimy tile. His stomach lurched but he didn't go in, just used the adrenaline to keep moving. Michael broke the surface for the last time and Danny could see one of his arms around the boy. The body. Jesus God, was it a body or a boy.

Michael reached the edge of the pool. He was coughing and spluttering, trying to keep both their heads clear of the water. Danny reached down and dragged the dead weight of the boy over the edge of the pool. He overbalanced and crunched onto the floor. He scrambled up on his hands and knees and reached out for Michael but he was already climbing out of the pool and reaching for the wee boy. He looked like he might be in primary school, no older than ten or eleven. His skin was an awful drained colour. Both of them had been cut by the glass and Danny could see blood ribboning down their faces.

He watched Michael give the boy the kiss of life. They

should have been at Robbo's by now. They shouldn't even be here. His ears popped and he could hear the slap of trainers coming closer on the concrete slabs outside. The other boy from the roof. Danny should be running or moving or doing something. He should be calling for help. Michael's phone would be fucked, he'd have to be the one to call for an ambulance. He fumbled for his mobile, unlocked it and pressed nine three times. It wouldn't connect for several long moments and in the silence he heard Michael exhale into the boy's lungs and push down with violent strength on the place where his heart should be. Danny heard a rib crack at the same time as a voice in his ear asked *What service do you require?* and he wanted whatever service would get him out of here the fastest.

He couldn't look away from Michael mechanically pumping air into the boy's lungs and forcing his heart to beat. Michael's face was turning red from the effort. It looked rounder than ever. The blood from the boy's head was thicker and darker now and it looked like something vital was going. Had he even moved by himself since he'd hit the water?

The boy's pal crashed through the door but stopped short at the shallow end. Like he couldn't believe what was happening. He just stood there, panting. What the fuck had they been doing on the roof?

If this was a TV show the scene would cut to an ambulance arriving but he had to wait instead, long minutes of watching Michael and listening to the voice in his ear telling him to *stay calm, someone's coming, they're on their way and they'll be here soon,* smelling the stink of piss and hearing the jagged breathing from the boy at the shallow end. The wee boy at the edge of the deep end didn't move once. Danny kept thinking he was moving but it was just what Michael was doing, the boy's arm would jerk or his head would roll to the side but it wasn't him doing it.

Michael kept going. There was a ringing in Danny's ears that turned into sirens and he could see blue flashes through the smashed glass on the front door. He tried to guide the paramedics in but they were already coming through the door and he watched them rush past him and the other boy. Michael kept going until they reached him.

Witness Protection

Kevin Cormack

In the shadow o waals
we must be gey winked wae hid—
kiddan wirsaels
every sup o the soup bowl
between the temples.
Or droondan in hid like buul-
heided Billick o the Ha.

Rattle the underworld,
expectan clemency?
Whit the unburied spirits widna gae
fur anither go at the hert, the duggid hert:
tarrie-fingered, ill-veetrit
and guttural as Tammick
o Greentaft's heirloom accordion.

They widna worry thumsaels
wae this clear broth racket,
or witness protection.

Contributors

Ian Alexander is a pen name whose owner lives in Edinburgh. He has previously been published in *Gutter*. @i_alex_ander

Eilidh Cameron is a writer from Edinburgh. She studied English Literature and French at the University of Glasgow and now works for Scottish Book Trust. Eilidh won the Janet Coats Memorial Prize for poetry at the 2023 Paisley Book Festival.

Regi Claire, Swiss-born, Scotland-based, was shortlisted for the Forward Prize for Best Single Poem 2020 and won the Mslexia and PBS Women's Poetry Competition 2019. Her fiction has won a UBS Culture Foundation Award and twice been shortlisted for Scotland's National Book Awards. She teaches at Edinburgh University. www.regiclaire.com

Natalie Jayne Clark is a neurodivergent poet, writer, and editor based in Perth, Scotland. She is a regular writer and editor for SNACK Magazine and Assistant Producer of

StAnza Poetry Festival. Her debut novel, *The Malt Whisky Murders*, is being published by Polygon early 2025.

Kevin Cormack is from Kirkwall and writes in Orcadian and English. His first poetry chapbook, *Toonie Void*, was published by Abersee Press in 2021. He also co-runs the music label Spillage Fete Records.

Andrew Cranston was born in Hawick in 1969 and lives in Glasgow. He studied at Gray's School of Art and at the Royal College of Art. His narrative paintings derive from literary and historical sources and from his own personal history. He is represented by Ingleby Gallery (Edinburgh), Karma (New York) and Modern Art (London).

Gill Davies is a radio/podcast/short film producer from Glasgow.

Sarah Davy is a writer, facilitator and mentor based in rural Northumberland. Her short fiction is published online and in print, and she won the Finchale Award for Short Fiction at the 2023 Northern Writers' Awards. Sarah is working on a short story collection exploring climate change in rural working-class communities.

Caoimhín de Paor is a writer from Cork, Ireland, now based in Edinburgh. His favourite medium is flash fiction, and he enjoys using it to explore memory and nostalgia. You can find him on instagram @Kevinjuly.

Wayne Dean-Richards has published fiction in magazines and anthologies. A collection of short fiction, *At the Edge*, and a novel, *Breakpoints,* was published by Spouting Forth Ink. Additional works include *Cuts* and *A Box of Porn*, with Kalman Dean-Richards, *Money & Blood* (Culture Matters Co-operative Ltd) and *It's A Mad World But Funny* (Outsideleft). @WDeanRichards

Gemma Elliott lives in Glasgow and works in local government. She has most recently published short fiction in *Neon*, *Crow & Cross Keys*, and *Truffle Magazine*.

Diego Espíritu was born in México in 1990. He is part of the research and creation collective Arte+Ciencia of the UNAM. He teaches the expanded literature course 'Máquinas post-concretas' on visual and concrete poetry and is the author of *Poemas Panks para community managers* and *the strange blue incandescence of mites*. www.diegoespiritu.com

Ian Farnes is a writer of prose and poetry from Burntisland, Fife who now lives in Barcelona. Alongside his writing he works as a literary translator, translating from Spanish into English. More information about his work can be found on his website ianfarnes.com

Holly Fleming is a writer from Glasgow and a graduate of English, Journalism, and Creative Writing from the University of Strathclyde. She enjoys reading and writing poetry and horror, enjoys being creative in any form, and currently works in marketing.

Martin Geraghty is a writer from Glasgow.

Laura Givens lives in Kansas City, Missouri. She has worked a variety of jobs, including house painter, union organizer, massage therapist, and civil servant. She has been taking writing classes through thi wurd since 2021.

John G. Hall was founding editor of radical arts magazine *Citizen 32*. His latest book *Making the Dark Visible* is published by Some Roast Poet publications, Manchester UK. He currently runs the Manchester Beat poetry night 'Beatification'.

Jon Russell Herring is a literary translator living in London. He was awarded the first Queer Digital Residency at the Poetry Translation Centre in 2022, and was a joint winner of the Stephen Spender Prize for poetry translation in 2023. *Quartet* is his first publication as a creative writer.

David Harrison Horton is a Beijing-based writer, artist, editor and curator. More of these poems can be found in his collection *Maze Poems* (Arteidolia). He edits the poetry zine SAGINAW.

Dom Howell is originally from Nottingham and now rents a place in the south side of Glasgow. He's had work in *Razur Cuts* and *Product Magazine* and he's working on a collection of short fiction.

Craig Johnson was born in New Zealand in 1972. He has published one book: *Sand to the Arabs: Memoirs of a Serial*

Salesman. The act of writing makes Craig feel truly at home with himself. He is currently completing his first novel *Mawg*.

Sneha Subramanian Kanta was the author of the chapbook *Ghost Tracks* (Louisiana Literature Press, 2020). She was the recipient of the inaugural Vijay Nambisan Fellowship 2019. She was Charles Wallace Fellow writer-in-residence (2019-20) at The University of Stirling. She is the editor of *Parentheses Journal*. Website: www.snehasubramaniankanta.com.

Simran Kaur is a freelance translator. She is also a writer with an interest in life, work, and relationships under capitalism and exploring possibilities for the future.

Chris Kinghorn is from Bathgate but now lives in the east end of Glasgow. He studied at the Royal Conservatoire of Scotland and has worked in the Scottish film industry for over a decade but his passion lies in literature.

Nicole Le Marie is from Fife but moved to London to follow a career in journalism. Her poetry and fiction has appeared in publications such as *Poetry Scotland*, *Lallans*, *Firewords*, *Dear Damsels*, *Salome* and has been shortlisted for the Bridport Prize. She enjoys experimenting with the sounds and language of her childhood home.

Sophie Leslie is based in Glasgow, Scotland, after a period of living, studying and working in Scotland, England, Paris and Brussels. Twitter handle: @sophleslie

Kik Lodge writes short fiction in France where she lives with a menagerie of kids, cats and rats. Her work has featured in *The Moth, Tiny Molecules, The Cabinet of Heed, Milk Candy Review, Reflex Fiction, Ellipsis Zine, Splonk, Bending Genres, Janus Literary* and *Litro Magazine*. Erratic tweets @KikLodge

Gillian Mayes is an academic (now with honorary status) in the School of Psychology at Glasgow University. She lives in the west end of Glasgow. As well as having academic publications, she has written numerous short stories and been published by thi wurd and in *New Writing Scotland, Ten Writers Telling Lies* and *Postbox Magazine*. She is the author of a campus novel as well as a novella.

Pamela McLean is a writer and librarian from Glasgow.

Sean McMenemy was born in Paisley in 1988 and now lives in Glasgow. An ex-footballer, barber, and taxi driver, he took up writing five years ago. His stories have been published in *The Honest Ulsterman, Southword* and *Creeping Expansion*.

Alan McMunnigall was born in Glasgow and grew up in the Sighthill area in the north of the city. He founded thi wurd in 2006.

Tatora Mukushi writes fiction and non-fiction, hailing from Zimbabwe and living in Glasgow via London. He is a human rights solicitor and gets his inspiration from his two golden children.

Joe Murphy was born in Dundee in 1979 and has been writing for most of his life. The classes run by Alan McMunnigall were, and remain, hugely influential. These days he lives in Ayrshire with his partner and their two girls and writes whenever he gets the chance.

Derek Murray is a writer and artist currently working on a novel. An exhibition of his paintings is scheduled for 2024 entitled "Nattkörning". Resident artist and team BKN member at Björkö Konstnod, Norrtälje. He lives in Stockholm, Sweden.

Eugene O'Hare is an Irish author and actor. His plays, most recently *The Dry House,* are published by Methuen Drama. Poems have appeared in thi wurd, *Causeway/ Cabhsair, Gutter, Dreich Magazine, Stand Magazine* and more. He is working towards a first collection.

Mel Piper is a writer based in Coventry. Mel's work focuses on bringing the weird into the everyday, and has previously been shortlisted by Sleek City Press. She has run workshops for adults and children. Outside of writing, Mel is also a keen photographer, with work featured in multiple publications.

Anjali Ramayya started writing poems and stories following her recent retirement from a career in psychiatry and medical software development. Inspired by life in India and Scotland, the two countries she calls home, her work has been short/longlisted in competitions and published by *Poetry Scotland, Dreich Magazine,* and *Writers' Umbrella.*

Maggie Reeve was born in Manchester, brought up in Leeds and studied Visual Art in Sheffield and The Slade, London. After many years teaching art in Glasgow she began writing, discovered thi wurd and now gets inspiration and encouragement by attending their classes and events. She has had a number of stories published by thi wurd.

Lorna Robertson was born in Ayr in 1967. She studied at Duncan of Jordanstone College of Art in Dundee and currently lives and works in Glasgow. Her densely coloured paintings, often made with a combination of oil paint and collage, sit somewhere between abstraction and figuration. She is represented by Ingleby Gallery (Edinburgh).

Matthew David Scott is a writer from Manchester. His first novel, *Playing Mercy*, was long-listed for the Dylan Thomas Prize; and he was a finalist for the Rhys Davies Short Story Competition. The co-founder of theatre company, Slung Low, Matthew's work has been performed both nationally and internationally. He lives in Newport, Cymru.

Megha Shah is a Mumbai-based aspiring author and a student of Psychology. You'll find her reading a book when she's not busy surviving academia. She heads her university's creative team, has a penchant for the exquisite mundanity of literary fiction and hopes to write her own novel someday.

Catriona Shine is an Irish-Norwegian writer and architect. Her debut novel, *Habitat*, longlisted for the McKitterick Prize 2022, was published by The Lilliput Press in March 2024. She is a recipient of an Arts Council Literature Bursary Award. Her work has appeared in *The Dublin Review*, *Aesthetica Magazine* and elsewhere.

Jerry Simcock, a retired teacher in a child psychiatric hospital and other settings, lives in East Lothian and spends his time writing and making art. *Giselle and Mr Memphis*, his first novel, was published by Vagabond Voices in 2022. A second novel, *Billy Tuesday*, is slowly taking shape.

Gerry Stewart is a poet, creative writing tutor and editor based in Finland. Her poetry collection *Post-Holiday Blues* was published by Flambard Press, UK. Her poetry appeared as part of the iamb poetry project and on the Eat the Storms poetry podcast in 2022. Her writing blog can be found at http://thistlewren.blogspot.fi/ and @grimalkingerry on Twitter.

Carl Thompson is a Glasgow-based writer and editor.

Joanne Thomson is an actor, writer and director from Glasgow. As a Royal Conservatoire of Scotland graduate and a BAFTA LA Newcomer, she has acted on some of the UK's most-loved stages, worked across BAFTA-winning series and has directed internationally award-winning theatre. This is her first foray into prose. www.joannethomson.co.uk

Joe Waite was born in Lancashire, and now lives in Glasgow with Holly and their daughter Joss. He loves working as a stroke physiotherapist, getting out into the mountains, and off-kilter stories about community.

Bechaela Walker is a Glasgow-based writer and Educational Coordinator for the Workers' Educational Association. Her stories have been published in *New Writing Scotland* and *Gutter*, and by The Common Breath, thi wurd, and Monster Emporium Press.

Debra Waters writes short stories and flash. She won the Bridport Prize (Short Story) in 2020 and was highly commended for Writers & Artists Working-Class Writers' Prize (2022). Shortlists include: Bath Short Story Award, the Bridport Prize (Flash Fiction), Pat Kavanagh Award. Longlists include: Manchester Fiction Prize, London Library Emerging Writers Programme.

Mandy Watson is a former NHS Clinical Scientist for whom early retirement, due to ill health, provided an opportunity to explore her creative side. She is a member of Garnethill Writers' Group, has published in *From Glasgow to Saturn* and has recently completed her first novel.